When the Cherry Blossoms Fell

Jennifer Maruno

Napoleon

Cover art and design by Vasiliki Lenis / Emma Dolan

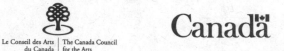

Le Conseil des Arts | The Canada Council
du Canada | for the Arts

We acknowledge the support of the Canada Council for the Arts for our publishing program.

We acknowledge the financial support of the Government of Canada through the Book Publishing Industry Development Program (BPIDP) for our publishing activities.

Napoleon Publishing
an imprint of Napoleon & Company
Toronto, Ontario, Canada
www.napoleonandcompany.com

Printed in Canada

13 12 11   5 4

Library and Archives Canada Cataloguing in Publication

Maruno, Jennifer, date-
        When the cherry blossoms fell / Jennifer Maruno.

ISBN 978-1-894917-83-4

1. Japanese Canadians--Evacuation and relocation, 1942-1945--
Juvenile fiction. I. Title.
PS8626.A785W48 2009   jC813'.6   C2009-900682-0

Dedicated to
Eiko Kitagawa Maruno.
Arigato.

One

March 1942

When Michiko arrived home from school, her father's square black case waited on the hardwood floor beside the front door. She sighed. It meant he was leaving. She had hoped he wouldn't go before her birthday. Next week she would be nine.

Itsamu Minagawa, "Sam" to all his friends, was a travelling salesman. His leather sample case carried a selection of fine chocolates and candy. The Imperial Confectionary Company of Canada was sending him on the road again.

The late afternoon sun streamed through the diamond-shaped panels of red glass in the front door. It gave the two cranes on the silk panel hanging above the hall table a rosy glow. Michiko placed her school books on the table, next to a black enamel vase. It looked like it held bare branches, but she knew they would soon be bursting with colour. Her mother was always coaxing something into bloom, even while the landscape slept.

Michiko entered the living room and flopped into a wide-winged armchair. Her small brother Hiro sat on the carpet next to the piano, banging a wooden spoon against a metal rice pot. Her mother was playing, while her father, in the matching chair, clapped in time to the music.

Michiko gnawed at the tip of her long, dark pigtail. "How long will you be gone?" she asked her father.

"Only a week," he replied. "The children of the world are running out of candy."

Michiko didn't return his smile. She needed to talk to him about something that had happened at school that day.

She glanced around the front room of the brick bungalow she had lived in since she was born. On the mantle was a collection of photographs. She knew her mother and father had lived in a different part of Vancouver before she was born. Michiko wondered if that was what the girl at school had meant when she'd told Michiko her family should go back to where they came from. Did the girl think her family should move back to the old neighbourhood, where Aunt Sadie and her grandfather still lived?

Michiko thought about the delicious smells that wafted out of the restaurants in that part of town. She loved to peer into the shop windows at the rows of women pedalling sewing machines, or watch the printing press stamping out wide sheets of paper. The only thing she didn't like were the tubs of fresh fish, knowing they were about to become someone's dinner. She always wanted to tip the barrels and set them free.

Finally, her father Sam hitched up the leg of his pants and kneeled before Hiro. He stroked Hiro's little round face, mussed his hair and planted a kiss on top of his head. "Goodbye, my little Peach Boy," Sam murmured. Then he looked up at Michiko and winked.

Last night, her father had told her the tale of a boy born from a peach. He tried to convince her that Hiro had come from a giant peach they'd found at the market in Japantown. Her father was always teasing.

Eiko, her mother, removed the sheets of music from the piano ledge and placed them inside the bench. She wasn't wearing the same clothes she'd had on at breakfast. She had changed from her cornflower print dress and apron into a pink wool skirt and matching sweater. Around her neck lay a single strand of perfectly matched pearls.

Michiko knew there was no time left to talk with her father. She also knew her mother wouldn't explain properly. All she ever said, whether Michiko asked about the blackouts, or the broken windows down the street, was "These are terrible times."

Eiko removed Sam's heavy wool coat from the closet and held it open for him. He was proud of this coat, hand-tailored and made to measure. The first time he'd worn it, he told Michiko there was a nose hidden inside, and she shook her head in disbelief. His heavy lidded round eyes sparkled when he showed her the label. Stitched in yellow, across the grey silk rectangle, were the words Matsumia and Nose, Quality Clothes. He'd pulled her inside and wrapped it around her as they'd laughed at his joke.

Now Sam slipped in his arms and buttoned it up. He removed his dark felt fedora from its peg and placed it firmly on his head. Then he picked up his case. "Goodbye, Eiko," Sam said. He kissed her on the cheek. Then he kissed Hiro and Michiko. His breath smelled of mint candy. "Take care of yourselves," he whispered.

Michiko followed him out on to the verandah. The scents and colours of their front garden were hidden, the lawn and hedge dusted with snow.

Her mother stood in the front bay window to watch and wave. The sleek black Ford with its long square snout pulled down the driveway. Its whitewalled tires reminded Michiko of her father's mints. She watched until the car was out of sight.

"Will he be back for my birthday?" Michiko asked when she came inside.

Her mother nodded. "He's never missed it yet."

* * *

It rained most of the time her father was away. The snow disappeared.

Michiko spent a lot of time after school drawing at the kitchen table. She used to attend Japanese school before dinner, but it had closed. Michiko didn't mind missing the Japanese history lessons, but she did miss the writing lessons. She enjoyed holding the big heavy brush, learning how to make the large strokes of the *kanji* on sheets of newspaper.

Crayons of every colour littered the kitchen table. Michiko practiced drawing umbrellas. Each day, her teacher selected a student to record the weather, and most of the children drew raindrops. One boy just scratched his crayon across the paper and said it was a puddle. Michiko wanted to draw something special. As she drew a Japanese umbrella, Michiko thought about the place where her father and grandfather were born. *One day I will visit Japan,* she decided.

The doorbell rang. Michiko dropped her crayon and ran down the hall.

Her aunt backed inside, closing her bright red umbrella behind her. Her high-heeled shoes left small puddles on the hardwood floor. Parking her umbrella in the enamelled stand, Aunt Sadie placed a large paisley satchel on the floor.

Michiko hoped Aunt Sadie would be staying over. When she was around, everything became fun and glamourous.

Sadie put down her satchel and removed her raincoat. Over her grey, pencil-thin skirt, she wore a long-sleeved white blouse with frills down the front. A red velvet bow peeped out from her collar, above the long row of pearl buttons. Her lips and nails were the same colour as the bow.

Sadie turned to the mirror and admired her hat. "Pretty, isn't it?" she said. She lifted the thin dotted veil away from her eyes and pushed the box of black feathers with red tips upward and off. "I bought it in San Francisco," she announced, handing it to her niece. "Mr. Maikawa got me a deal. I only paid $2.98."

Michiko thought her aunt was the luckiest woman in the world. Not only did she work in a dress shop, she got to travel with her boss and his family. She knew so much about the world.

"Don't tell me you paid three dollars for a hat," Eiko exclaimed as she greeted Sadie with Hiro on her hip. He was newly awake from his nap, and one of his chubby cheeks still held the red imprint of a crib bar.

"I wanted it," Sadie responded with a shrug. "So I paid it."

Michiko cradled the hat as if it were about to fly away. She raised it a bit to look at the sides. *A cake,* she thought. *It looks like a cake of feathers.* She turned to her mother and said, "This cake isn't just as light as a feather, it's made of feathers."

Both women stared at her.

"Your niece has quite the imagination," her mother responded, "like someone I know."

Eiko lowered Hiro to the dining room carpet, and Michiko sat down beside him. Eiko entered the kitchen and returned with a small tray. She set it on top of the white embroidered tablecloth. On it were two black lacquered bowls filled with miso soup. There were small bowls of crisp yellow radish, small green puckered pickles and rice. Michiko had eaten her lunch in the kitchen with Hiro while her mother had made *manju*. It was the special treat she always made for Michiko's birthday. Her mother formed soft white balls around a spoonful of sweet red bean paste then dusted them with powdered sugar.

Michiko watched the two women slide into their chairs. They had similar oval faces, blue-black shiny hair and soft almond eyes. She knew, even though they looked alike, that they were very different.

Her mother wore her dark hair in a perfectly pinned bun, never a hair out of place. Her aunt's hair, cut in bangs, was level with her ears. Her hair always swung and flew about her face when she talked. And Sadie talked a lot. She flounced into a room, she laughed loudly and always said what she was thinking.

Michiko's mother said very little. She entered a room quietly and spoke softly. She never argued or offered an opinion. She usually made herself invisible.

Eiko lifted the small iron teapot from its stand. She poured pale green tea into two small blue bowls and handed one to her sister.

"When do you expect Sam back?" Sadie asked.

"He will be home soon enough," Eiko replied confidently.

Michiko jumped up. "He has to be home tonight," she insisted. "Tomorrow is my birthday."

"That's right," Sadie said with a smile, "nine years old tomorrow." She glanced at the small stack of gifts on top of the piano. "I hope we don't have to wait until your father gets home before we open your presents."

"He's just a little late," Michiko's mother announced. "It's so rainy. The roads can be bad."

"That's not all that's bad out there," Sadie declared. She put her teacup down and leaned across the table. "Did you know...?"

Eiko flashed her a warning look. "Not now, Sadie," she said. She nodded in the direction of the children.

Then she smiled at Michiko. "He will be here in time."

Michiko entertained Hiro with the toy monkey her father had brought her from his last trip. After she wound the key in its metal back, the monkey hopped about on his front feet and curly tail. He banged his two cymbals together. Each time they clashed, the small bell on his tiny red hat shook and tinkled. Hiro's eyes lit up, and he clapped his hands.

Sadie flipped through a magazine as the clock on the wall ticked. No one spoke until the shrill ring of the phone broke the silence.

Michiko watched as her mother held the receiver to her ear. She spoke only once. Her face paled as she listened. Then she lowered the receiver, almost missing the two large claws that held it in place. Michiko watched her sink onto the chesterfield beside her sister.

Something was wrong. Instinctively, Michiko pulled Hiro onto her lap.

Sadie looked up from her magazine. "What's going on?" Seeing her sister's face, she threw the magazine on the floor.

Eiko's eyes brimmed with tears. She wrapped her arms around her waist and rocked back and forth.

"What's happened?" Sadie asked as she put her arms around her sister. "What's wrong?" Her eyes pleaded for an answer.

Finally Eiko mumbled a few words. Sadie had to lean in close to hear.

"What?" Sadie exclaimed shrilly and sat bolt upright. "Sam is in jail?"

Two
Blackout

Sadie cancelled Michiko's birthday party. Strangers filled their home instead of her school friends, and all they talked about was the arrest. Eiko served everyone tea, and they ate all the *manju* that was supposed to be for the party. Michiko watched and listened. Her Japanese wasn't good enough to understand everything that was said. Every now and then, her mother put down the teapot and stared off into space.

At the end of the day, the small stack of presents on top of the piano remained unopened.

That night, Eiko sat on Michiko's bed studying her fingers. Michiko pushed her storybook across the bedspread and nudged her mother with it. Eiko picked up the book and put it on her lap. The pages fell open.

"Don't read that one," Michiko whispered. "I'm saving that one for Father." She flipped the pages forward. "Read this one instead."

Her mother stood up, paying no attention. The book fell from her lap to the floor. Instead of picking it up, she went to the window and adjusted the drapes.

"It's too late for me to leave," Sadie announced, strolling

into the bedroom. She plunked herself on the end of the bed.

"I think," Eiko told her sister, "you should stay here from now on."

Michiko was glad her mother had asked Sadie to stay. With her father away, their house seemed big and empty.

Sadie looked at her sister. "It would be better than bunking down with the livestock at Hastings Park."

Michiko giggled. Why would her aunt think about sleeping at the Exhibition? It didn't even open until the summer. She could almost feel the hot July sun and remembered wading into the noise and smells of the Exhibition. She couldn't wait to hear the mechanical music of the rollercoaster and smell the bright pink cotton candy.

Last summer, they'd taken Hiro to the fairgrounds. He'd loved the sheep, even though the sawdust had made him sneeze. He brought home a yellow balloon. At the fishpond, Michiko won a red celluloid bird on a stick that flapped its wings in the breeze. She thought about how much fun it would be to live at the fairgrounds.

Michiko clapped her hands. "I'd sleep in one of the Giant Dipper's carts." She turned to her mother and smiled at their joke. "The roller coaster seats are padded."

Aunt Sadie nodded. "Good idea, but the midway section is locked." Then she added, in a quiet voice, "In case someone gets the same idea."

"Do you have any food to bring?" Eiko asked.

"No," Sadie responded.

Eiko shook her head and said, "With shops closing down, it's getting harder to find the things we like."

"I've got lots of cash. I sold everything."

"Everything?" Eiko asked.

"Everything," Sadie said. "Even my red feathered hat. In fact, I sold that for exactly what I paid." She patted her hair, as if the hat were still on her head. "Just think, I wore it all that time for free!"

Suddenly, Michiko pictured her Aunt Sadie sitting on a stage, wearing her red feathered hat, surrounded by flowers and blue ribbons. "You'll never win a prize at the Exhibition now," Michiko murmured, shaking her head.

Both women stared at her, but this time they did not laugh. They did not even smile.

"Maybe I should let some things go," Eiko suggested.

"Good idea," Sadie agreed. "These days, you never know what's going to happen next." She took her sister's hand. "I'll help you make a list."

Michiko retrieved her book from the floor and placed it back on the shelf. The noise of a key in the door in the front hall made them all freeze and look at each other in silence. Michiko pushed her way between them and ran down the hallway.

Three men crowded into their front hall. Only two of them faced her, but Michiko knew the coat, the hat, and the back of the neck of the third. She especially knew that straight black hair.

"Daddy," she screamed.

He turned quickly and gathered her into his arms. The shoulder of his coat was damp. It smelled like the coarse wool of the lamb at the fair. Did her father sleep with the animals? Was it true what her aunt had said about Hastings Park?

"Hello, my little princess," he murmured into her neck.

Her mother, carrying Hiro, came to his side.

Sam put Michiko down. He cocked his head to one side and looked at his little son. He smiled and cocked his head the other way. Hiro's face broke into a big grin, and he put out his arms. His father took him into his and hugged him. He gave Eiko a kiss on the lips.

Michiko looked at her aunt in surprise. She had never seen her father do that before. He only ever kissed her mother on the cheek.

The men patted her father on the back and left, closing the door behind them, but, just as the family settled themselves in the living room, there was a second knock on the door. Sadie yanked it open. A man with clear blue eyes above a brown walrus mustache stood on the stoop. His black hat glistened with small drops of rain.

"Sam left this in the car," he said, holding out a small square cardboard box. Sadie put out her hands to take it. She grimaced. The bottom of the box was damp. The man tipped his hat and closed the door.

Seeing the box, Sam laughed. "It's Michiko's birthday present." He put his hand out and tugged one of her braids. "You didn't think I would forget your birthday?"

The rough brown string that held it together had several knots in it. He broke the string and lifted out a small round bowl of shiny turquoise gravel. A fat golden fish with two bulging eyeballs fluttered its long translucent fins.

"I'm going to name him Happy," Michiko said. She threw her arms about her father's neck. "I'm so happy you are home."

Hiro reached out his fat little hands, opening and closing his pudgy fingers. "He wants to pick it up," Michiko told her father. "He probably wants to put it in his mouth." She placed it on top of their four-legged radio stand, away from the grasp of her small brother.

Back in bed, Michiko snuggled against her father's strong shoulders. "Promise me you won't go away any more," Michiko pleaded.

"I can't promise you that," he responded. "You know I must work." Her father's eyes took on the same faraway look that her mother's had worn the other day. "In fact, I will be going away again, soon."

Michiko pouted.

"You must promise me one thing," he said, drawing her close to his side. "Promise me, that no matter what happens, you will help look after your family."

Michiko thought for a moment. "Aunt Sadie can look after herself," she retorted. "She tells me that all the time."

"I know," her father told her. "But I am counting on you to look after the others."

Michiko bit her upper lip. Then she rolled over and faced the wall. Her father tucked the covers in around her. She didn't want her father to leave again, ever.

It seemed as if she had slept the whole night, but it

was still dark when Michiko opened her eyes. She pulled back the covers and stepped into her slippers.

The nightlight in the hallway was out. It was another blackout. She hated the blackouts, even though the boys at school said they liked them. She stepped into the hall.

Muffled voices came from the living room.

"I am very lucky," she heard her father say. "I could have been sent straight to the Pool."

Michiko rubbed her eyes. Why would her father think he was going swimming? She crept further down the hallway. She knew it was *yancha* to eavesdrop, but she wanted to know what was going on.

"Why did they stop you?" she heard her mother ask. "You had your registration card, and you were on company business."

"I had a map," he replied.

"A map?" Sadie cried out. Both Sam and Eiko shushed her. "What kind of map?" she whispered.

"Paul Morrison, one of the guys at work, drew it." Michiko heard her father's giant sigh. "He was showing me where his aunt Edna lived. It's near one of my favourite fishing spots."

"Near the Kootenay River?" Eiko asked.

"He drew it so I could visit next time I went fishing." He sighed again. "It was just a simple scrap of paper. I can't believe how much trouble it caused."

"How did anyone know you had it?" asked Eiko.

"It fell out of my pocket when I stopped to buy the goldfish." He sighed again. "The owner of the pet store must have reported me."

"Stupid goldfish," Sadie berated. "It should be named Trouble instead of Happy."

Michiko raised the tips of her fingers to her mouth. Sadie was not being nice.

"Thank goodness Mr. Riley vouched for me," her father said. "He said that if they took me away now, he would make trouble. He has a business to run."

Michiko silently clapped her hands for Mr. Riley. He was the likeable man who was her father's boss. Last year he'd given her a china tea set for Christmas.

The talking stopped. Michiko turned to go back to bed, but the voices continued. She paused again to listen.

"I have to go, you both know that. The government's ordered all Japanese-born men out."

No one spoke.

Michiko tried to imagine what these men of the government looked like. Why were they ordering her father out? Out of where?

"Sadie," Sam asked, "what will you do?"

"I'm staying right here from now on," Sadie replied in a whisper. "It's not safe where I live. Besides, Eiko will need my help. Sisters stick together."

"Thanks," Michiko heard her father say. Then he asked, "And what about Geechan?"

"My father will be difficult," her mother said. "He thinks he is strong enough to work alongside the others." Eiko sighed. "He's waiting to be called, but they won't take him. He's too old."

"You all must stay together," Sam said. "I will talk to him." There was a long moan as he stretched. "Let's get to bed," he said. "We need all the rest we can get."

Michiko scurried back to her bed and huddled to the side by the wall, fearful of giving herself away and frightened by the strange conversation.

Three

Only Ten Days

Sadie studied her niece's picture. "You are turning out to be quite the artist," she said before shoving the crayons to one side to make room for the teapot.

Michiko grimaced.

"Say thank you," her mother admonished.

"Thank you," Michiko mumbled. She wanted to finish the picture she was making for her father. It was her favourite part of the story of Peach Boy.

Geechan, her grandfather, handed her mother the morning mail. He lived with them now, like Sadie. Hiro's crib was in Michiko's room, and Sadie and her mother shared a bed. Having Geechan around helped Michiko forget that her father was in the mountains. He always wore a smile on his wrinkled chestnut face.

Eiko opened a letter. After scanning it for a minute, she said, "Ted's written to tell us about his big plans."

"Our brother always has big plans," complained Sadie.

"He says that since he's lost his boat, he's leaving Port Rupert."

"How did Uncle Ted lose his boat?" Michiko asked in surprise. "Did he forget to anchor it? Did it float away?"

Her mother did not answer. She continued to read the letter silently. "He's found work," she said instead.

"Where?" asked Geechan.

"I don't know exactly," her mother replied. "He says it's somewhere in the interior."

"He can't build boats in the interior," Sadie scoffed. "What is he up to?"

Eiko read aloud. "The owner of the shipyard, Mr. Masumoto, is the building supervisor. I am one of the carpenters he is taking along." Her mother stopped reading. Michiko could see her eyes scanning the words. Then she continued. "We will help to build a new hospital, along with," she paused, "several small houses."

"Several small houses," Sadie added. "You know who they are for, don't you, Eiko?"

Eiko shrugged, folded the letter and returned it to its envelope. She placed it in the pocket of her apron.

She never reads the entire letter out loud any more, Michiko thought. *She only reads bits and pieces to me. She has even stopped letting me read them on my own.* There were so many secrets and mysteries in their house these days.

Michiko thought about her goldfish's new home on the window sill. Where had the slim wood cabinet with the curved legs gone? She had loved to open and close the two big ivory knobbed wooden doors when the radio was not in use. Some of their beautiful hangings and paintings were no longer on the walls, and their cabinet of blue porcelain vases was almost empty. The camera had disappeared, and no one tried to find it.

Geechan took Michiko by the hand. The skin of his hands was paper-thin and the bones birdlike. He led her to the kitchen door and pointed to the cherry tree in full bloom. "We have only ten days," he told her.

"Why only ten days?" Michiko asked.

"Cherry blossoms open all at once," he explained. "In Japan, the petals last only ten days."

"But that's in Japan," Michiko protested. "This is a Canadian tree. It will bloom longer."

Geechan sighed. "A cherry tree is a cherry tree," he said, letting go of her hand.

Michiko decided to keep track of the days, the way they did at school. On the calendar, she drew a cherry blossom. She would draw a blossom each day the tree was in bloom.

She felt Geechan's hands on her shoulders. "What day will we have our *hanami?*" he said into her ear. She could smell his strange mix of soap and fish.

"What's that?"

"In Japan, people celebrate the opening of the cherry blossoms." He opened his arms wide. "They have picnics under the trees."

Michiko's eyes lit up. She turned to her mother. "May we have a *hanami?*"

Her mother lifted her hands from the bubbles in the sink and wiped them on her apron. "We only have one tree," she said. Then she smiled at Geechan.

"Let's have a picnic under the cherry tree," Michiko pleaded. "Please." She tugged at her mother's apron.

"I suppose I could make *sakura-mochi,*" Eiko said. "If

I could find the right ingredients."

"I'll find what we need," Sadie piped in. She sat with her feet on a chair, flipping through a magazine. "I know a few people still in business."

This would be a very special picnic if her mother was willing to make cherry rice cakes. "Did you hear that, Hiro?" Michiko ran to her brother, propped up in his high chair by a purple pillow. "We are going to have a *hanami*."

She looked into his bowl. Several toast fingers covered a floral design. Michiko grabbed the bowl and dumped out the toast. "Look," she held it up. "It has a cherry blossom on the bottom."

Hiro blinked. His tiny pointed chin quivered, and his round fat face turned red. He opened his mouth wide and howled. Two large teardrops popped on to his cheeks.

"Sorry," mumbled his sister as she picked up the toast bits and put them into his bowl.

Hiro smiled through his tears. He clumsily picked up one of the fingers of toasted bread. "Ha," he grunted and crammed it into his mouth.

"That's right, Hiro," Michiko prompted him, "ha-na-mi, say it Hiro, ha-na-mi."

Hiro crammed a finger of toast into his mouth and reached for another.

Geechan tapped the calendar. "Saturday," he said. "Our *hanami* will be Saturday."

That would be the eighth day of blossoms. Michiko looked out the kitchen window. A few petals lay on the grass. She ran outside and gathered them up.

On Saturday afternoon, Sadie and Geechan spread a futon on the grass beneath the pink blossomed branches. Her mother carried out a large pink china plate. Outlines of cherry blossoms, etched in gold, danced along the edge. They drank green tea from small cups shaped like lotus flowers and feasted on *sakura-mochi*, butter tarts and thin slices of sponge cake.

Geechan brought Happy outside, and Michiko fed him a few crumbs of cake.

"Now it is time for the entertainment," Sadie announced. She daubed the corners of her mouth with a napkin, then she rose from her knees and straightened the skirt of her special occasion *kimono*. Sadie extended her hand to her father. "I bring you *Hanaska-jiisan*, the story of the old man and the cherry tree."

Geechan pulled a red silk scarf from his pocket. He tied it around his forehead. From his other pocket he pulled a red tin flute.

Michiko's mother gasped. She pressed her fingertips to her lips and opened her eyes wide. She gathered Hiro onto her lap and pulled Michiko to her side. "We are going to hear a *rakugo*," she told the children.

Sadie told the story in Japanese while Geechan played the flute. Eiko quietly whispered the translation in their ears.

Michiko watched her aunt's face glow as Geechan's fingers danced up and down the tiny holes of the flute. While her mother whispered, he made the flute sing.

First, Sadie told them of the miserable old man who sat under his cherry tree every day. Geechan played the flute slowly then made a mean face. She told them he wouldn't allow anyone else to sit under the tree, even when it blossomed.

Then their mother said, "While eating cherries, the old man swallowed a pit." Geechan collapsed into a fit of fake choking. Michiko and her mother laughed.

When he sat up, a small branch stuck out of his headscarf. Michiko understood that a cherry tree now grew from the top of the old man's head.

She listened carefully and guessed at parts of the story. "Everyone made fun of him because of the tree in his head," she said to Hiro. Her mother nodded.

Then Geechan rose up. With great effort, he pulled the branch off and collapsed sideways.

"He pulled the tree out of his head," Michiko said excitedly.

Geechan reached for a small bowl. He placed it on his head. He walked about the yard, balancing the bowl and playing his flute at the same time. Sadie danced about him, fluttering her fingers up and down around him.

"Auntie Sadie is showing us rain," said Michiko. "Did the hole in his head fill up?"

Her grandfather sank to the ground. He put down his flute. He took the small glass bowl from his head and picked up the goldfish bowl. He walked about the yard holding the bowl with Happy on his head.

"The hole in his head became a fish pond," Michiko's mother told her.

From behind the tree, Sadie took out a stick with a string. She dangled it over the bowl.

"She's pretending to fish," Michiko shouted. "Did she catch it?" Her mother nodded. She placed her finger on her lips for a quieter ending.

Sadie removed the fishbowl, and Geechan jumped up. He pretended to be mean and angry. He felt the top of his head. His hand went down his neck and along his back. He slumped and rolled behind the tree.

Sadie put the fishbowl where he sat and told them what had happened in Japanese.

Eiko whispered, "The mean old man turned himself inside out trying to find his fish, until he ended up at the bottom of the pond. All that was left was water."

Michiko and her mother clapped their hands. Hiro looked about and copied them.

Geechan came out from behind the tree and took a bow. Sadie folded her hands and sank to the blanket.

They sat quietly as the soft early evening breeze caressed their faces. A few petals floated onto the blanket. Hiro yawned. The breeze grew stronger. Suddenly they were in the midst of a flurry of white blossoms.

"*Sakura fubuki*," Geechan announced. He held his hands out to let the petals slip through his fingers.

"That's right," her mother said, "a cherry blossom snowstorm."

"Looks like I can still bring down the house," Aunt Sadie bragged.

Everyone laughed. To Michiko, it seemed as if the cherry tree were laughing too. Her only wish was that her father had been there with them.

Four
The Locomotive

Michiko felt like an overstuffed sausage. Sadie had insisted she wear as much of her clothing as possible to save space in their luggage. First, she put on her sleeveless sundress with the large pockets. Over it she wore a green plaid dress with puffy sleeves. Then she buttoned her long sleeved white cotton blouse over the top and stepped into her new navy wool skirt. When her arms went into the sleeves of her brown hooded coat, the shoulders bunched. She carried her blue straw hat with the white daisy by its elastic string.

The great black locomotive hissed and groaned as the stack churned out white smoke.

Eiko lifted the two cases at her side and moved towards the car in front on them. Michiko gripped her aunt's heavy paisley carpetbag and followed.

The conductor, the angular cheekbones of his face showing through his pale white skin, stepped down. His eyes narrowed as Michiko and her mother approached. He shook his head and held up his hand. With the other, he pointed down the track.

They walked past a few cars and stopped again. The

same thing happened. Each time they tried to board the train, someone moved them along.

Her mother gave out a long sigh. She glanced back at Geechan in his best black suit and tie, wearing his bowler hat. He could not walk fast, having insisted on carrying the large *furoshiki*. The great square cloth held their bedding. There was a brand new quilt inside, one Michiko's mother had worked on diligently since her father had left.

"Is something the matter with our tickets?" Michiko asked. Her mother gave her a tired look and didn't answer.

Finally, they found their train. It sat back from the others, off to one side. The rusty, peeling, old engine towed only four cars. Three were passenger cars. The last car looked like a large wooden wagon. It was for the baggage.

Only Japanese people were aboard, all sitting up straight, staring ahead.

Michiko stepped over the railway ties onto the black oil-stained gravel. She tiptoed to keep her shiny black patent shoes clean.

They mounted the stained wooden steps, just as the train's big iron wheels spun in place. It shrieked, puffed a billow of steam and jerked forward. Michiko stumbled and banged her knee. Someone caught her by the elbow and steadied her. Several people shuffled seats to let them all sit together. Michiko plopped down hard on one of the wooden benches just as the train moved forward.

"Where are we going?" Michiko asked for the third time that day. This was a very strange way to travel.

Usually they went on vacation in their father's car.

Eiko undid the pearl buttons of her pink wool jacket and took Hiro onto her lap. "To the country," she said. She busied herself arranging Hiro. His hand reached for the grey grosgrain band of his mother's felt hat. She tucked one of his hands beneath her arm. The other she put under the blue satin trim of his blanket. "We will be near the mountains," she added.

"Father's mountains?" asked Michiko hopefully.

"He's in a different part of the Rockies," was the response.

"Why are we going away?" Michiko asked.

"The city is too crowded," her mother said quietly. "We will be vacationing in a farmhouse. The fresh air will do us good."

Sadie laughed. "That's a good way to put it, Eiko," she said. It looked as if Sadie hadn't followed her own good advice. She wore a light silk dress under a green duster coat and carried a matching purse. Her hat looked like a spring garden.

"Sshh," Eiko said, putting a finger to her lips. "No more questions. The baby is going to sleep."

Sadie looked at Geechan. His eyes were shut. "Which one?" she whispered and winked at Michiko.

This time Michiko put her finger to her lips. Her Aunt Sadie was fond of making fun of people, but Michiko didn't like it when it was Geechan.

She turned to watch the station pass. Crowds of Japanese women and children waited at different points along the tracks as their train lumbered by. It puzzled her as to why so many Japanese people were here. For some reason it made her feel sad. She pressed her face to the glass but pulled back. Dead flies scattered the sill.

Michiko gave a great sigh. She wished they didn't have to take this vacation. She didn't want to go to a farmhouse in the mountains. She wanted to go to Japan instead. She wanted to see the places her father and Geechan talked about, the places where they were born.

The train picked up speed, past the tall grey buildings, then it moved into a shadowy forest. Huge black-spined firs towered over the tracks. Clouds of sumac peppered with seedpods flanked the rails. The train wound its way along the rim of a gorge, and Michiko stared down into a small canyon laced with tiny waterfalls. She felt as if she were travelling through her storybook. Sadie and her mother closed their eyes.

Feeling hungry, Michiko dragged the carpetbag out from under her seat and pushed the wide wooden handles apart. As she opened the clasp, she felt someone watching her.

A frail woman stood next to her sleeping mother. Her small arms stuck out of the short sleeves of her blouse. Several long white hairs escaped from the bun at the nape of her neck.

Michiko lowered her eyes. The woman's tiny sandals and ankle socks gave her little girl feet. She looked up just as the woman smiled, displaying missing teeth and black gums. With a crooked finger, she stroked Hiro's cheek. Then she gazed directly into the carpetbag.

"*O-bento?*" the old woman asked, looking at the

small packet of sunflower seeds and the orange.

Michiko shook her head. It was only a snack. She shut the bag with a thud. Then, she turned her shoulders and stared out the window until the woman moved away.

The rest of the people on the train were silent. She listened to the rhythmic pounding of the wheels on the track. Her eyes closed as she felt the train speed up and slow down many times over. Finally, Michiko rested her head on her mother's shoulder.

When she awoke, a large, shining lake filled the window beside her. There was a sandy beach along the edge. She dipped her head down to look at the high blue-topped mountains across the water. The pearl buttons of her mother's suit jacket were once again in a perfect row. Michiko glanced around. Geechan was gone, and so was Auntie Sadie. The railway car was completely empty, except for the three of them.

"Are they here?" came a woman's loud voice, followed by heavy stomps up the wooden steps. "Are they here?"

Down the aisle stomped a large red-faced woman in a bright print dress. She wore a yellow straw hat brimmed with cherries on top of a pile of curls the colour of carrots. Several of the cherries had chunks missing. Their insides looked like mothballs.

The woman's cheeks were bright pink from exertion. Her lips, painted with heavy lipstick, were the same color as the cherries. She put her hand on the back of a seat to steady herself and catch her breath. "Mrs. Minagawa?" she asked, blinking behind round gold spectacles.

Michiko's mother nodded and stood up, holding

Hiro. Michiko waited.

"I'm Edna Morrison," the woman announced. Her voice was loud and strong. It made Michiko think she was angry, but her face was smiling. "What a sweet little boy," she exclaimed. She put out her arms to take him. "He looks just like a little doll," she said.

Hiro whimpered. His lower lip protruded, his mouth opened wide, and he wailed.

"Oh my," the woman said in surprise and moved back. "Oh my, my," she repeated. "I guess everyone is a little out of sorts."

The woman took Michiko's mother by the elbow. "Come with me." Michiko grabbed the carpetbag. "We've got a ride."

A huge pile of duffle bags and trunks lay in the dirt beside the steps. Mrs. Morrison stepped around them to the green pick-up truck parked by the depot. A man in a dark flat cap slouched against the front bumper. He wore denim farm pants and a red plaid shirt. His neck was tanned deep brown, the same V-shape as his open shirt neck.

Sadie waved from the back of the truck. "Welcome to the Land of No," she called out.

Mrs. Morrison hauled herself into the front seat. Eiko tried to hand Hiro to her, but he clung to her neck and wailed. Eiko walked to the back of the truck and passed him up to Sadie. Sadie gave him to Geechan, who sat perched on the edge of his suitcase. Their belongings formed a pile in the middle.

Sadie hauled Michiko up into the back of the truck.

"What did you call this place?" Michiko asked.

"The Land of No," her aunt explained. "No streetcars, no buses and no cinemas."

"There's electricity and running water," Eiko said. "That's what's important."

They watched the train gather steam as it came to life again. The driving rods pushed the large black wheels out of the station, chugging uphill, then all went quiet.

The pick-up truck rocked and swayed along the dusty dirt road. Michiko rode standing with her back pressed against the cab as it climbed the steep mountain. They passed people from the train. All of them carried sacks on their back and suitcases in their hands. They made their way down a narrow rutted lane, between the trees.

"Where are they going?" Michiko asked.

"To their new homes in the woods," her aunt replied, pointing up the lane.

Michiko swivelled her head. She couldn't see any houses. All she saw was a huge hill, covered with pines. She looked straight up, to find the sky.

"There is no limit to looking upward," Geechan told her when she lowered her eyes.

Michiko thought about living in the woods. "Do you think there are bears?" she asked him, but the wind swallowed her words. She turned quickly to her mother to ask again but didn't; her mother's face was like a mask.

They passed large wooden houses with railed verandahs. It seemed strange to see houses spaced so far apart, without fences. They passed green fields blooming with tall spikes of flowers that looked just like paintbrushes.

On they drove, past a small white wooden church with a bell tower and tiny cemetery. The truck lumbered over a narrow wooden bridge where a stream raced past banks of waving bluebells and daisies.

When the truck finally left the dirt road and turned onto a large winding lane, it sped up. The wooden sides of the truck rattled, and the floor shook. Michiko's hat began to flap. Her mother covered Hiro's face with his blanket. Then Michiko's blue straw hat blew up, across the back of the truck and away on the wind.

Five

Be Grateful

The truck slowed to a crawl and turned off the main road, where a rusty red iron gate stood ajar. In dark carved letters, the sign on the corner post read NELSON. The road ahead dipped down and split. Michiko could see a long, low white building at the bottom with mountains looming behind. Battered board fences framed the fields on either side.

Mrs. Morrison waved her plump freckled arm out the window. "This is it."

Their four-hour ride in the back of a truck had finally ended.

The man in the flat cap got out. He removed the pipe from between his brown stained teeth and used it to point at the old wooden farmhouse. At one time, the house had been dark green, but it hadn't seen paint in years. A cluster of small stunted trees that reminded Michiko of old men stood close together down one side. Clumps of grey brush grew up and onto the long thin wooden verandah. The golden matted field reminded Michiko of the prize cow she had seen at the Exhibition.

Mrs. Morrison beckoned to Michiko, but she backed

away. She did not like the sickly sweet smell of the loud woman with the cherry hat. She took Hiro, while Sadie helped Geechan down.

Michiko watched the driver and her mother talking. It was a good thing he spoke with her and not her grandfather, she thought. Most people had a hard time understanding him. He mixed his English words with Japanese. Michiko knew it was because Geechan was *Issei,* like her father. But her Mother, Aunt Sadie and Uncle Ted had all been born in Canada. They were *Nisei.*

Her mother removed a thick white envelope from her purse. She took out a paper and handed it to the driver. He read it, nodded and handed it back to her. Then she handed him the envelope. He removed his cap, placed it inside and put his cap back on his head. Then he got back behind the wheel beside Mrs. Morrison. *He isn't going to help us carry anything inside,* Michiko thought.

"Thank you, Mrs. Morrison," her mother called out with a wave. She nudged Michiko to wave as well, but she didn't.

As they approached the house, two squirrels gossiping at the end of the verandah ran off. They mounted the long plank steps, and Geechan pushed open the wooden door. A tarnished metal lantern hung from a nail beside the frame. The clattering of their shoes echoed over the wooden floor.

They entered one large room on the ground floor. There weren't any walls to divide the space into living room, dining room and kitchen. A set of stairs ran across the back, with a row of wooden pegs on the wall behind it. There was a sink and a counter. A large red-handled metal pump stood over the sink, with a washboard propped on its side against it.

Across from the counter was an ugly, black iron monster stove. Geechan carried Hiro to the stove and patted it. *"Hee-ta,"* he told Hiro, and together they peered into the large wooden box next to it, brimming with logs.

A small, square pine table sat on top of a patch of linoleum in the middle of the floor. There were four kitchen chairs, each one a different shape and colour. A corn broom stood in the corner next to a tin bucket. A thick strip of brown tape hung from the ceiling, matted with the bodies of flies. The entire place had a deep musty smell.

Michiko's mother looked around and gave a small sigh. "So, this is our new home," she said, removing the long pearl-tipped pin that fixed her hat to her head. Taking her hat off, she pushed the pin back into the brim and placed the hat on the table. She gave a weak smile.

"New?" Michiko retorted, looking around in surprise. "This isn't new." There wasn't even a couch or stuffed chair. Where was she supposed to curl up and read?

Sadie fumbled with the window above the sink, attempting to open it. Spiderwebs filled the corners on the outside, and a fat bumblebee lay still in the corner inside the frame. She flicked it onto the floor with a look of disgust. "It's nailed shut," she complained. "This is so *inaka.*"

"You are right, Auntie Sadie," Michiko said. She stood

in the middle of the room with her hands on her hips. "Why are we spending our vacation in this old place?"

Eiko placed her hands on Michiko's shoulders and guided her to one of the wooden chairs. She pulled another out and placed it in front of her. Then she sat down and took both of Michiko's hands. "We are very grateful for this house," her mother told her in a low voice.

Michiko furrowed her brows. How could her mother be grateful for a house like this? It wasn't anything like the one in the city.

She looked past her mother. The front door was nothing but one big wooden plank. Their door at home was dark mahogany, with an oval frosted window. In the middle of the pane, there was a tulip. Its petals were made of the diamond-shaped panels of red glass, outlined in copper.

"Do you know how lucky we are?" her mother asked.

Michiko did not respond. She was busy thinking about the door. It had a knob of chipped enamel and a wooden peg at the side to keep it shut. The knob on the door at home looked like a huge cut diamond that she liked to pretend was a real jewel. Their door locked with a key. This one didn't even have a keyhole.

"Michiko." Her mother spoke sharply, giving her shoulders a shake. "Do you know how lucky we are?"

Michiko moved her gaze to her mother's face, surprised at the tone of her voice.

"Mrs. Morrison helped us make these arrangements." Her mother's voice trembled as she spoke. "Some people have to live in tents until they have a place, but we have a whole house just to ourselves."

Michiko closed her eyes. The sharpness of her mother's voice upset her. Eiko did not usually speak that way to her, and Michiko didn't want to listen any more.

Eiko lowered her voice to a whisper. "Be grateful, Michiko, our whole family is together."

"Our whole family is *not* together," Michiko said. She broke free of her mother's grasp and stood up. "Father isn't here, is he?" She turned and ran up the stairs.

The first room at the top of the stairs had a small cot and a crib. Except for two bars, the paint on the rest of the crib was chipped and faded. Michiko plunked herself down on the cot. Two rough grey blankets lay folded at the foot of the bed. *This must be my room,* she thought. The springs below the thin worn mattress screeched. She bounced a few times to listen as she looked up at the ceiling. A long piece of string dangled from the single electric bulb with an enamel cuff. There were no sunburst swirls of white stucco like the ones on her bedroom ceiling at home.

She removed her coat, unbuttoned her blouse and stepped out of the wool skirt. She looked around. There was no closet. She took off the green plaid dress and folded her clothes into a neat pile on top of the blankets.

"Ted," she heard Auntie Sadie shout.

Michiko raced down the stairs.

Her uncle was so tanned and bronze, his arms looked bigger. He opened them wide, and Michiko ran right into them. "I haven't seen you since Christmas," she yelled.

Ted picked her up and twirled her about the room.

Then he put her down and staggered about. "You weigh a ton," he said, clutching at his heart. "How old are you now, fourteen?"

"Oh, Uncle Ted, you are so silly," Michiko giggled. "I'm nine. I just had my birthday."

Ted walked to Geechan and bowed. Geechan returned the bow with a nod of his head. Then Ted kneeled in front of Hiro, who was sitting on his grandfather's lap.

"Be careful," warned Sadie. "He's not a happy baby today."

Ted tickled his nephew under his tiny pointed chin. "Hello, Hiro," he said, "hello."

Hiro looked at his uncle and gave a shy smile. Then he turned and buried his face in his grandfather's coat.

"Good boy," Michiko's mother said.

"Yeah, you didn't howl," said Sadie.

"Have you got all of your luggage?" Ted asked.

"We weren't allowed to bring much," Eiko responded. "Bedding, pots and pans, the few dishes and clothes that we could carry. I could only ship two things."

Ted turned to Michiko. "Did you bring me a present?" he asked.

"Your present is our safe arrival," Sadie scoffed.

But Michiko had an idea. She dashed over to her carpetbag, took out her orange and put it behind her back. "Close your eyes," she told her uncle as she walked towards him, "and put out your hands."

Michiko placed the bright lopsided ball in them. "Now you can open your eyes."

For a moment, Michiko didn't understand the look

37

on her uncle's face. She thought, at first, that he was going to cry. Then he lifted the orange to his nose and drank in the pungent aroma of the peel. "Thank you, Michiko," he said, giving her a hug. "I can't remember the last time I had an orange."

Over his shoulder, Michiko could see her mother's face. She was smiling, and Michiko knew that she would be *yasashi* with her again.

"So what have you been eating lately?" Sadie asked Ted.

Ted bent his arms upward to flex his muscles. "Potatoes, potatoes and more potatoes," he said. "I'm desperate for a bowl of *miso* soup."

"We all are," retorted Sadie. "Goodness knows where we'll get Japanese food out here."

Six

Houses in the Orchard

Michiko hauled off her cotton nightgown. Yesterday's clothes lay on the floor in a pile. Her mother hadn't put clean ones out for her. She pulled on her long-sleeved blouse and buttoned it up before stepping through the elastic waist of her wool skirt. This is what she usually wore to school. It felt odd wearing school clothes on a summer vacation.

Michiko wiped the fine dry dust of the road from the toes of her shoes. She slapped her socks against the foot of the metal bed to rid them of the brown rings before putting them on. Hiro stirred. She picked up her shoes and tiptoed downstairs.

The rough wooden surface of the kitchen table lay bare. Where was their embroidered cloth? Two small red enamel bowls sat alone with a pair of chopsticks across them. One bowl was half-full of rice, the other of green tea.

Michiko lifted the bowl of snowy white rice to her face to breathe in the sweet aroma. It was cold. She looked around. Where was the bowl that held her egg? There wasn't even *shoyu* on the table. Michiko always dribbled the dark soy sauce on top of the thick yellow yolk. Then she stirred the large staring eye with her chopsticks and poured it over the hot steamy rice. *This is a very plain breakfast,* she thought. She poured some of the cold green tea over her rice and gave it a stir.

"*Ohayo,*" her grandfather called out, hearing her move in the kitchen. He sat on the verandah in a wooden chair facing the sun, whittling. "You slept a long time, my little cherry blossom."

"Good morning," Michiko said as she moved to the steps to put on her shoes. The sun was bright, but the air was cool. She was glad of her long-sleeved blouse and warm skirt.

She walked to one end of the verandah and leaned on the railing, facing the field of crumpled grey grass. The other side of the dirt road was dense with trees.

"We should be grateful," Geechan said.

Now Geechan is saying it, Michiko thought as she turned to him.

Geechan gestured to the right with his knife. "We have an orchard," he told her. "Next spring, we will have a grand *hanami.*"

Michiko glanced at the rows of short, gnarled trees sprouting small green leaves and shrugged. *Geechan doesn't understand we are only on vacation,* she thought. But he often didn't understand things about their life. He lived the same way he used to live in Japan, and Sadie complained about it a lot.

She heard her mother's and aunt's voices coming from the side of the house and went to investigate.

Sadie was busy tying a rope between two of the

small, stunted trees. A large white apron covered her denim overalls and red plaid shirt. A red silk kerchief kept her shiny black hair in place. Only her short straight bangs showed. Michiko was used to seeing her mother in an apron, but not her aunt.

The two women stared down at the large galvanized tub in front of them with their hands on their hips.

As Michiko approached, she stepped on a branch, hidden by pine needles. It made a loud crack, and both women looked up.

"Ahh, the princess is awake," Sadie said. "But you are not Princess Minnehaha, a true daughter of the forest." She lifted a finger to her lips. "You make too much noise when you walk."

"What are you doing?" Michiko asked, ignoring her aunt's attempt at humour. She stared into the tub.

"Diapers," her mother responded as she picked up the tin bucket at her feet and dribbled water down the side of the washboard. "We are washing Hiro's diapers."

Sadie threw in a large yellow brick of soap, but it did not sink to the bottom as Michiko expected. "The water is still cold," Sadie complained as she swirled it around in the water. "We should have heated it longer."

"We can do that tomorrow," Eiko said. "Let's get these done, or Hiro won't have any diapers at all."

Sadie took one of the diapers from the small basket on the ground. She plunged it in and out. Holding the yellow brick, she rubbed the two together. "Too bad you didn't ship the washing machine," she said as she plunged the diaper in again, "instead of the sewing machine." She rubbed the diaper up and down the washboard, plunged it in once again and gave it a hard wring. Then she handed the white twist to Eiko.

Eiko plunged the diaper up and down in the bucket. She too gave it a hard wring. Then she walked to the rope and draped the diaper over it.

"Is Hiro awake?" she asked.

Michiko shook her head.

"I'll go in," Eiko said, removing her apron. "You can take over the rinsing." She draped her apron over a branch.

Michiko couldn't believe her ears. What did her mother want her to do?

Auntie Sadie held out the white twisted roll. "Come on," she said. "You'll get the hang of it in no time."

Michiko put two fingers into the pail of water and quickly pulled them out. Aunt Sadie was right. The water was freezing.

"I can't wash clothes in this skirt," she complained. "I'm not even allowed to play in it. It's for school."

Sadie laughed aloud. "School?" she echoed. She tossed the diaper into the bucket. Then she grabbed her sister's apron from the branch. "Raise your arms."

Michiko obeyed.

Sadie wrapped the apron around her chest. She tied it at the back then in the front. "Put it in fast," her aunt directed. Then her voice softened. "I know the water is cold."

Michiko plunged in her hands. She swished the diaper about, then she pulled it up out of the water. She swished it around again. She thought her hands would turn blue, but they only went bright red. She held the diaper over the bucket and let it drip.

Her aunt snatched it up. She gave it a good hard twist, and water streamed out. Then she handed Michiko the twisted roll.

Michiko took it to the clothesline. She tried to arrange the diaper over the rope the same way as the one beside it. It almost fell into the dirt, but she caught it in time. She flipped it across the rope. Then she wrapped her hands in the hem of the apron and held them between her knees to warm them.

On the way back, Michiko stepped on the same stick, and it cracked again. The stick looked like a large fork. Michiko picked it up and stripped off the bark. She wiped it on her apron and stuck it in the pail, using it to swirl the diaper.

"Good thinking, princess," her aunt complimented.

Michiko was hanging the third diaper when her mother came outside. Hiro stretched out his fat little hands. Michiko removed the apron and took him in her arms.

From her pocket, Michiko's mother brought out a handful of wooden pegs. They reminded Michiko of tiny people without arms. Her mother pegged the diapers to the line.

"You keep Hiro entertained," she mumbled past the peg in her mouth. "I'll finish the washing."

Michiko shifted her little brother to her hip and looked down into his chocolate brown eyes. "Well, Prince Hiro," she cooed, "when will your royal baby carriage finally arrive?"

Hiro grinned and gurgled.

Michiko sidestepped the path that led to the small grey hut. The smell of lye and lime and the wooden bench with the round hole disgusted her. Last night was the first time she had ever used an outhouse. For once, Michiko wished she could wear diapers too.

She made her way down the rutted road, shifting her brother from one hip to the other. The weathered building at the bottom of the road reminded her of a barn, even though it wasn't barn-like in shape.

Across the front of the building, the ghostly outline of two pink circles rested on a bed of pale green leaves. Scrawled across the front, the faint peeling letters spelled out the word "Apples". A row of small square-paned windows, several panes broken, ran beneath. Short stubby planks covered some of the windows haphazardly. Skeletons of vines rattled against the flaking patches of grey wood.

The two large-planked doors stood ajar. Michiko gave one of them a push. It swung open with a creak, and she stepped into the shadowy space.

"Ooh," Hiro cooed. His eyes widened.

Once her eyes grew accustomed to the dark, Michiko could see long wooden benches against the walls. Broken wooden crates lay about an earth floor strewn with sawdust.

Michiko sniffed. She recognized the aroma. *Apples,* she thought, *I can smell the apples.*

The rays of sun streaming over her head rested on a new wall of yellow plywood. The sudden sound of several hammers pounding together startled her. Then the hammering stopped. Uncle Ted appeared from behind the wall.

"Well, well, well," he said, slipping his hammer into his belt. "Look who's come to visit." He took Hiro from her arms.

"Thanks," she said. "He's heavy." She wiggled her arms about.

"Hey, Tadishi," Ted called out, "come and meet my sister's kids."

The man who stuck his head out from behind the partition was wearing a white bandana with a red circle across his forehead.

"Michiko," Uncle Ted said, "this is Tadashi."

Tadashi, wearing a white undershirt and khaki pants with a rope belt, stepped forward and gave her a slight nod.

"He used to work with me at the shipyard," Ted explained. "He arrived from Japan recently," he explained. Under his breath, he muttered, "Very bad timing."

At first, Tadashi appeared to be the same age as Ted, but when he moved into the patch of sunlight, she noticed the shocks of grey hair above paper-thin eyelids that sagged and folded at the corners.

"What are you building?" she asked. She peeked around the corner but drew back suddenly. Behind the wall were two small metal bunks. The same rough grey blankets that she had on her bed were on these. Over one of them was the staring face of the Japanese Emperor Hirohito. *If Sadie saw that,* Michiko thought, *she would rip it down,* but she wasn't sure why her aunt disliked him so much.

"Is this someone's home?" She could see the top of a suitcase sticking out from under one of the beds. She had intruded. "I'm sorry," she mumbled.

"Sort of," her uncle told her. "We live here, while we turn this place into barracks."

"Barracks," Michiko repeated. "What's that?"

"A home for workers," Ted told her. "We are going to fill the orchard with houses, and we need more than two men to do it."

Michiko clasped her hands. They were going to build a neighbourhood. She had a vision of a street of houses like the ones in her neighbourhood.

"I'll show you," her uncle offered and led her to a wide makeshift table. He rolled out a long paper, placing his hammer on the curly edge to hold it down.

Michiko realized she was looking at a house with the roof off, just like the doll's house she had at home.

The drawing showed one big room, divided by two half-walls. Michiko placed her finger on the words and read them out loud. In each corner, small rectangles were labelled "bunks". A square in the middle read "cook-stove". A circle across from it read "heat-stove".

She placed her finger on a line with an arrow at the end of it. "Is this the front door?" she asked.

Ted nodded. "One house, two families," he murmured. "The government is so kind to us."

Before Michiko could ask what he meant, Hiro gave out a gigantic wail.

"He's probably hungry," she said. "He's always hungry."

As Michiko headed back to the farmhouse, she

hoped some children lived nearby. It would be nice to have someone to play with while they were on vacation.

That night, as she listened to the sound of crickets, the wind whispering through the pines and the hoot of an owl, Michiko began to wonder why two families would want to share a house. Why wouldn't they live in a house of their own?

Seven

Family Photographs

Trucks laden with lumber travelled back and forth in front of the farmhouse daily, turning the road into two deep muddy ditches.

Michiko made a calendar using the bottom of a cardboard box Geechan brought home. He looked for things of use wherever he went, never returning empty-handed. One day he brought a small enamel basin caked with mud. Another day it was an armful of burlap bags. Sometimes he returned with things to eat. Michiko loved the fleshy fan-shaped mushrooms he gathered from the woods.

When he presented a pailful of wild vegetables to Michiko's mother, she glanced into it and smiled. Auntie Sadie looked and grimaced.

"Where did you find them?" Eiko asked.

"*Dokodemo,*" he replied.

Michiko peeked in at the smooth green stalks with tightly coiled tips.

Geechan nudged her. "Try one."

She reached in. The strange green antennae were cool to the touch. Their coils were covered in short rusty-brown hairs. Michiko brushed away the hairs and bit into it. It was crisp and, to her surprise, sweet. "What are they called?"

"*Warabi*," he said, shrugging his shoulders. He did not know the name in English.

"They're called fiddleheads," Sadie piped up. "See how the end looks likes the head of a fiddle?"

Everyone ate the greens for dinner.

"We need to find out how we can dry them," Eiko said. "We could store them like mushrooms."

"Ask Mrs. Morrison," Sadie suggested. "That woman knows everything."

Mrs. Morrison had visited Michiko's family once a week since they arrived. Michiko soon came to recognize the sound of her black-laced shoes stomping up the verandah stairs. There would be a short pause before she knocked, in order for her to catch her breath.

Eiko made her black tea, knowing this new friend wasn't fond of the tiny twigs and leaves that floated about in the tea they drank. Mrs. Morrison sipped from the gold-rimmed china cup with pink roses that Eiko had packed. She nibbled on Ritz crackers served on the small green glass plate.

Each visit, Mrs. Morrison brought them something. She gave Geechan a pair of black rubber boots for his walks in the countryside. She won Hiro's affection by pulling an Arrowroot cookie from her handbag each time he sat on her lap. Sadie received a jar of cold cream. Eiko got recipes and advice, and Michiko always got something to read. Her favourite gift was the tattered gold embossed book *Fifty Famous Fairy Tales*.

Mrs. Morrison taught them how to keep the reservoir on the stove full of hot water for washing faces and hands. She showed them how to place the oval copper pot with handles over two stove lids to boil water, and put bricks in the warming oven to take to bed at night.

She let Geechan teach her how to use chopsticks, and to count to ten in Japanese.

The same man that picked them up at the station dropped her off at the top of the road on his way out of town. He never drove into the farmhouse lane, and he never got out of the cab.

"Would you like to invite your husband in for a cup of tea?" Michiko's mother asked.

"I would indeed," Mrs. Morrison replied, "but he is too far away to do that. My husband is with the troops. That's Bert, the farmer down the road, who brings me here."

"It seems we are alike," her mother murmured, "both waiting for our husbands to return."

Hearing the long, low sound of the locomotive passing by, Mrs. Morrison glanced at the slim gold watch embedded in her pudgy pink wrist. "Well," she announced, "school's out."

At the word "school", Michiko lifted her head. "I wish I was in school," she murmured.

"You *should* be in to school," Mrs. Morrison said. She peered over her little round gold spectacles at the little girl across the table from her. "Why aren't you?"

Sadie laughed. "She has to be the only child I know who would rather go to school than be on holiday."

"School holidays don't start for a while yet," Mrs. Morrison said. "She shouldn't be missing her studies."

"I didn't know if she would be welcome," Eiko said quietly.

Mrs. Morrison contemplated this until a honk came from the road where the green pick-up truck waited. "I'll look into getting you into school," she told Michiko. She clutched her purse to her chest and marched out the door. "Let you know next week."

Michiko hung her head. She hadn't meant that she wanted to go to school here. She meant that she wanted to go to her old school.

Her mother put a finger under her chin and raised it. "What is wrong now?"

"I want to go to school at home," Michiko cried and stamped her foot. "I don't want to be here one more day."

"A day is only a day," her mother said. "Even the most important days of all come and go."

"Like what?" Michiko demanded, tired of this vacation.

Her mother walked to the window ledge and lifted down a small rectangular parcel. She placed it on the table and untied its brightly coloured silk. "Look," she said, lifting the bamboo lid. "This whole box is full of important days."

Inside was a collection of papers and photographs.

Eiko sifted through the layers and handed Michiko a thick card with ruffled edges. "Here is an important day," she said. It was a black and white photograph.

Michiko hadn't seen this photograph before. The woman staring straight ahead was wearing a white kimono

51

and a boat-shaped headdress. The man next to her was all in black. He wore a long loose jacket over his kimono.

"This is a traditional Japanese wedding," her mother said. "Do you see the white embroidered crest on his *haori*?" Michiko nodded. "That is my family crest. The bride wears a *shiromuku*. Do you know who they are?"

Michiko shook her head.

"This is my *baachan* and *geechan*." Her mother stroked the faces of the bride and groom. "When my grandfather was a young man, he left Japan to see the world."

"Did he come to Canada?"

"He took a steamship across the Pacific Ocean to the United States." Eiko looked up from the photograph and smiled at Michiko. "He wore European clothes for the first time. Then he returned to his village to marry his childhood sweetheart."

"Why didn't you wear a *kimono* on your wedding day?" Michiko asked.

"I was a modern woman," her mother responded. She sifted through the papers and brought out the photograph of her wedding day. The edges of it were uneven and jagged.

Michiko remembered this picture in a silver frame, on top of the mantelpiece. "Where is the frame?"

"It was too heavy," her mother said quietly. "I left it behind." She took the photograph from Michiko. "I wanted a store-bought hat and coat for my wedding." She traced the folds of the gown. "But my mother wouldn't hear of it. She insisted on making my dress." Her eyes glazed over. "The church at the corner of

Powell Street was full. There was even a crowd of children hanging around the doors."

"That's because they wanted to see the baseball players. Your father knew everyone on the Asahi team," Sadie chimed in from the sink. "They were all at the wedding."

"Were there flowers?"

"Oh yes," sighed Eiko. "The church was full of them. She turned to her sister. "Do you remember, Sadie? I carried white lilies and scarlet snapdragons."

Sadie stopped drying the teacups. "I was the maid of honour," she said. "I wore a yellow dress. My hat had a little short veil at the back. It matched my dress perfectly." She sighed. "Our mother was a wonderful seamstress."

Eiko smoothed out a worn piece of newsprint. "Look, Michiko," she said, "this was what she drew first. Then she made the pattern." She held a faded pencil sketch of the dress in the photograph.

"That's where you get your drawing talent," Sadie remarked. "Your grandmother went to one of the most famous dressmaking schools in Japan."

Eiko traced the drawing with her finger. "Each sleeve had fourteen lace-covered buttons. Do you remember, Sadie?"

Sadie smiled. "I had to do them up." She mimicked wiping her brow. "There were thirty of them down the back."

"The women in your mother's class talked about that dress forever," Sadie told Michiko.

"My mother's class?" Michiko repeated.

Eiko rustled through the papers again and unfolded

a rectangular document with a dark green border and a shiny red seal in the corner. "My official certificate," she announced. "It's from the Kawano Women's Sewing School, in Vancouver."

Michiko peered at it. "Do you have one too?" she asked her aunt.

"We went to different schools," Sadie said. "I went to dancing school. Look," she said, "here's the newspaper article about your mother's school." She read from it out loud. *"Girls, it is noticed, come from all over the province to take courses in tailoring, dress design and dressmaking."*

Michiko picked up the photograph of her parents' wedding. "You wore your pearl necklace."

Her mother's fingers went to her throat. "Your father gave it to me as a wedding gift," she whispered. "The pearls came from a very special place."

"I know," Michiko cried out in excitement, "I know where your pearls came from."

"You do?" her mother said. "Where?"

"They came from Pearl Harbor," Michiko said with a smile. "I heard about Pearl Harbor at school."

Both women gasped. They looked at each other with wide eyes.

"No," her mother said crossly. "My pearls were harvested by the lady divers of Mikimoto." She packed up the box. "Your father had my necklace sent from Japan."

"Where is it?" Michiko asked. "Can I see it? Can I try it on?"

"No, you can't." Her mother looked at the picture in her hands. "It's gone."

"Did you lose it?"

Her mother did not answer.

Michiko wanted to know what had happened to the beautiful necklace. "Did someone steal it?" But her mother still did not respond. She placed the basket back on the shelf.

"She sold it," Sadie said finally. "She sold it along with the piano and everything else of value in the house."

"You sold your necklace?" Michiko stared at her mother with her mouth open. "Why?"

"I had to," her mother said. Then she slumped down in her chair and laid her head on her arms.

Sadie turned to finish the dishes. Michiko took one of her mother's hands and held it. She didn't know what else to do. There were tears on her mother's cheeks.

Suddenly Eiko rose and ran out the front door. Michiko went to follow, but Sadie grabbed her and held her back. "Leave her." She drew Michiko into a hug. "She hasn't shed a single tear till now."

Michiko looked into her aunt's eyes. They were brimming with moisture. "It's time your mother had a good cry." Sadie hugged Michiko harder. "It will do her good."

Michiko didn't want her mother to cry. She wanted her to wear the pearl necklace. Her eyes filled with tears as well.

Eight
School in Town

Ted showed them a small opening in the bush. "It's an overgrown trail," he told them. "The wagons took the apples to market this way." He pointed into the trees. "Follow it until you reach the road, then turn left."

Michiko trudged alongside Geechan. The hardboiled egg, nestled inside her tiny *furoshiki*, bounced against her leg. She had two rice balls and fiddleheads for lunch as well.

They pushed their way along the broken branches and grass. The trees seemed to close in behind them as they walked. Geechan had to duck under the low branches more than once. As they wound their way along the pine-scented path, the wind whispered through the needles. Michiko hoped they wouldn't meet a bear.

Part of the path followed a stream that trickled over the rocks and boulders. Michiko could smell the rotting marsh grasses. When the rasping call of a blackbird rose from the bullrushes, they waited to see the flash of red on its glossy black wing. The croaking and beeping of the frogs beckoned her to a game of hide-and-seek. She wished they could stop longer and watch for dragonflies.

Finally, they emerged from the bush onto the long stretch of dusty road. Thorny bushes covered with wild roses greeted them from the shallow ditch.

They passed a rutted laneway much like theirs, which led into a pasture dotted with daisies. The sound of hammering drifted up to the road. Michiko saw her grandfather's eyes drift longingly towards the sound. His hands were always restless. Her mother had once told her this was why he made such a good barber. When he wasn't cutting hair, he was whittling at a piece of wood.

When they reached the narrow metal bridge, Geechan stopped. Past the bridge was the town. Michiko leaned over the handrail to look at the willow that swayed above the river. Grey water rushed past below them with a roar.

Geechan gave her a small push. Michiko knew this meant she was to go on alone. She turned to her grandfather. "What if no one likes me?" she said in a low voice.

"Not like you?" Geechan's eyes crinkled at the corners when he smiled. "You are nice girl with a smart head. Why they not like you?"

Michiko took a deep breath and stepped off the bridge. She walked for a bit, then turned to wave, but her grandfather had not waited. He was off to the field of hammers.

She smiled. Uncle Ted often joked about his nine-man team. He said the government paid eight men for eight hours to put up a house. When Geechan helped, they took a longer lunch break.

One night at dinner, Ted had used chopsticks to

demonstrate how the little houses went together. "The posts go into the ground, and we lay the main beams," he said. "Then we put the floor panels down, and the walls go up." He told them how they built each wall with the door and window spaces right on the ground. Then they lifted the the wall and bolted it to the floor. After the stoves went in, they added the roof panels. The house was finished when they nailed the last panel down.

Several of her uncle's small square wooden houses with shingle roofs now stood in the orchard. Smoke from one of the chimneys curled up into the pale blue sky. *Maybe I will meet someone from those houses at school,* she thought as she walked into town.

The spaces between the large roadside maples grew wider. She spied the church steeple as she approached the square wooden buildings on the corner. *No buses, no streetcars, and no traffic lights,* she could hear her aunt say as she turned and made her way down the main street.

A soft fragrance wafted towards her. It came from a small tidy house with scrolls of woodwork around the porch. A picket fence separated the house from the street. The arched gate was overgrown with a cloud of lavender and ivory lilacs that filled the air with their perfume.

Michiko stopped in the middle of the road to breathe in the fragrance. It reminded her of the cherry tree in her own backyard.

"Hey," someone yelled, "move."

The sound of the bicycle bell made her jump. Michiko darted in the same direction as the rider.

"Watch out!" the boy on the bike yelled. He stomped

hard on his brakes. The bicycle wobbled and fell to one side. The boy fell off, and the bicycle landed on top of him.

Michiko could only stare at the brightly polished fenders and leather seat.

A boy got slowly up off the ground. He dusted himself off and looked up. "So, is it a dirty Jap that made me fall?"

"I didn't mean—" Michiko started to say, but he cut her off.

"Next time, I'll run you over." His cold blue eyes told her he meant what he'd said. He turned and picked up his bike.

Michiko watched the white-walled balloon tires turn the corner. She continued to walk, but when she turned the corner, the Union Jack was fluttering high on the pole. That meant school had started. She broke into a run, making her pigtails smack hard against the side of her face.

Out of breath, she pushed open the schoolhouse door. Without thinking, she slipped off her shoes as she did at home and stepped into the schoolroom, leaving her shoes outside the door. Thirteen pairs of unsmiling eyes turned her way. The teacher put down her piece of thick yellow chalk. Michiko waited in the aisle, not knowing what to do next.

"Come in," the teacher said.

Michiko moved forward.

A boy on the aisle looked down. "She ain't got no shoes," he exclaimed. "She must be even poorer than me."

Everyone laughed, and Michiko hung her head.

"Now, now, boys and girls," cautioned the teacher.

"She must have shoes. Her socks are a lot whiter than any of yours."

Several children bent to examine their own socks.

"Put your shoes back on," the teacher directed Michiko kindly. "We don't take our shoes off here."

Michiko returned and thankfully slipped them back on. The coolness of the dark linoleum floor was already seeping through her socks.

"Come up to my desk," the teacher said. She sat beside a clay pot of scraggly geranium plants. "My name is Miss Henderson," she said softly. "You must be the little girl Mrs. Morrison came to see me about."

Michiko stood before her, her hands at her side. She didn't know what to say.

"What is your name?" the teacher asked.

Michiko whispered her full name. "I am Michiko Takara Minagawa."

"Please say it again," the teacher requested. "I didn't quite hear you."

Michiko whispered it a second time. The teacher shook her head.

"Maybe she's Italian," someone from the back offered. "Maria didn't know English when she first came."

"Write your name for me, please," Miss Henderson directed as she pushed a piece of paper towards her. Michiko picked up a pencil and wrote her name.

"She better not be one of those yellow bellies," a different voice from the back piped up.

The teacher looked up and frowned. "That's enough," she said. She looked at Michiko's name for a minute and picked up the pencil. She crossed out some letters and wrote down some new ones. She examined the paper for a moment, then looked up at the class. "We have a new student," Miss Henderson announced. She focused directly on the boy with the bike. "Boys and girls, meet Millie Gawa."

"Hello, Millie Gawa," they chorused.

The teacher pointed to a desk in the second last row. "You can sit beside Clarence."

"Hey, Clarence," a boy in the back called out. "Looks like you finally got yourself a girlfriend."

Miss Henderson clapped her hands loudly. All went quiet.

Michiko slipped into the seat beside the boy named Clarence, who looked as if he had been born on the sun. Red hair fell about his freckled face in curls. His large ears, rimmed with sunburn, stuck straight out like the open doors of her father's car. His nose peeled. Clarence wore a long-sleeved plaid flannel shirt and brown corduroy pants. One of the buttons on the cuff was missing. The corner of the pocket was slightly torn.

Her mother would never have let her come to school like that, Michiko thought. She'd let down the hem of Michiko's cotton skirt, washed it, and dried it. Her white blouse was spotless.

They spent the morning writing out addition questions and multiplication tables. At recess, Michiko stood with her back to the wall, watching the children coo like pigeons over the green and ivory bicycle leaning against the wall.

"It's the New Elgin Deluxe," one of the boys called out to the others.

Its owner patted the silver mound between the two handlebars. "This is an electric beam," he boasted.

Clarence came late into the yard, returning the coal bucket from the small stove to the shed at the back. The sun tinged his red hair with gold as he closed the shed door with the toe of his boot.

At lunchtime, Miss Henderson asked Michiko to remain inside, while the others spilled out on to the wooden trestle table in the side yard. She gave Michiko a few words to spell and several passages to read. Then they ate their lunch together in friendly silence.

After lunch, the class had a botany lesson. The teacher directed them to sketch a flowering plant. If they wished, they could use watercolors to enhance their drawing. Michiko's eyes shone when the students passed back pieces of drawing paper. She found that drawing often helped her to ease her fears. Her joy diminished, however, when she opened the green enamel box. Most of the cakes of colour were gone. Those left had large holes in the centre, and the white enamel of the box's bottom showed through.

Clarence watched her sketch a long stem with small buds. Below, she drew clusters of small-petal blooms.

"That's good," he said. "It's a lilac, right?"

Michiko looked up, but he turned back to his work.

"Prepare for dismissal," the teacher announced.

Michiko blew gently on her paper before slipping it inside her desk.

"No leapfrogging across the desks," Miss Henderson warned the boys at the back as the children crowded towards the door.

Michiko raced along the hard dirt road until she reached the wooden bridge. Then she slowed down to walk the rest of the way. School had not been anything like the one she went to at home. She didn't know how to tell her mother that she had a new name.

At home, she slapped her *furoshiki* on to the kitchen table, laid her head down and closed her eyes. Her mother moved her hands to retrieve the bundle.

"What are these small cuts on your fingers?" Eiko asked. "What have you been doing?"

A bundle of thorny dark green stems and small pink roses fell out of the *furoshiki*.

Michiko opened her eyes. "The teacher said," she mumbled, "if you pick flowers and hang them to dry, they will keep their colour." She closed her eyes again. "We always had flowers on the table at home."

Nine

A Boat Called Apple

Everyone is to begin on page one," Miss Henderson directed as she handed out the papers. "Work as far as you can."

The class groaned as their day began with an arithmetic test.

Michiko twisted her braid before she started. She whizzed through the first page. It was all addition and subtraction questions. She turned the page. Clarence, she noticed, was counting his fingers inside his desk.

She completed the second page of multiplication and division questions and moved on to the third. It was word problems. After reading the first, she gazed across the room. Miss Henderson smiled at her. Michiko lowered her head to make a small drawing to help solve the problem.

A sudden sting on the back of her head made her jerk upright. Clarence picked up the bit of crumpled paper that bounced on to his desk. He slid it inside and unfolded it. His face flamed redder than his hair.

Michiko looked behind her. The boy with the bike smirked at her. Clarence ripped the note in half and stuck it in his shirt pocket.

"Put your papers on my desk on your way out," Miss Henderson directed.

The girls skipped but didn't invite Michiko to join. She stood and watched until Miss Henderson emerged from the school. As she waved the hand bell, Clarence ambled up to her side.

"I always wait until the rest have gone in," he told her. "That way nobody pushes you." He waited with Michiko until everyone was inside before he spoke again. "Most of the students dislike George," he told her. "Try to stay out of his way."

"Millie," the teacher called out as she entered the classroom. "I've marked your arithmetic paper. Well done. I'm moving you up a grade. You are to sit beside George from now on."

Michiko's eyes darted to Clarence's as she picked up her notebook and pencil. She moved to the desk beside the boy who owned the bike, took a deep breath, sat down, and smiled.

His clear blue eyes narrowed as he looked at her. "Are you one of those Dirty Japs?" he whispered.

"What did you say?" she asked.

"I asked if you were a Dirty Jap," he repeated.

Michiko heard him clearly that time.

George stared at her, waiting for something to happen. But Michiko couldn't think of anything to say. She flipped through the pages of the textbook. She would have liked to have said something, if she only knew what.

*   *   *

At home Michiko talked about her day at school. "A boy in my class called me a Dirty Jap," she said to her mother's back as she prepared dinner.

"And what did you say?" Eiko asked without turning around.

"I didn't know what to say."

"What is a Dirty Jap?" Michiko asked, moving to her mother's side.

Ted and Sadie overheard as they came into the kitchen.

"Did you do or say anything to this boy to make him angry?" her uncle wanted to know.

Michiko shook her head. "After the arithmetic test, the teacher made me sit beside him."

"That means he's jealous," Sadie said. "He was used to being the smartest in the class until you came along."

"Why did he call me dirty?" Michiko asked. "Even the teacher complimented me on my clean socks."

Ted pulled her into his arms. "I'm afraid in the eyes of some people, all Japs are dirty."

"Especially Hiro, when he fills his diapers," Sadie said loudly. She laughed heartily.

"*Shizukani,* Sadie," Eiko cautioned her. "This is why I didn't want her to go to school." She leaned against the sink. "I could have taught her here."

"With what?" Sadie retorted. "We don't have any books. Besides, she should know what is going on."

Sadie pulled Michiko away from Ted. "Listen, Michiko," she said, spinning her around to face her. "The lesson you learned at school today wasn't about arithmetic. It was current events."

"Stop it," Eiko cried.

Sadie ignored her. "Canada is at war with Japan after Japan bombed Pearl Harbor in the United States," she continued. "For some reason, people think all Japanese people are enemies."

Michiko's eyes widened. "Enemies?" she repeated.

"That's why we left Vancouver." Sadie stopped holding Michiko and relaxed her arms. "Everyone who was Japanese had to move away from the coast. It is the law." She slumped into a chair. "We left before they threw us out."

"Stop it," cried Eiko. "Stop it, Sadie."

But Sadie didn't stop talking. Her voice grew louder, as if she were telling a whole roomful of people. "The government made new laws for the Japanese every week. We weren't to have cameras or radios. Then we couldn't have cars or boats."

Ted walked away to look out the window.

"We couldn't go to certain stores. Japanese children couldn't go to public schools or use the libraries. They even shut down the schools that taught Japanese culture and language."

Michiko raised her fingers to her mouth. It was the government that had stopped her lessons in calligraphy?

"First, they took your uncle's boat," Sadie exclaimed, "then they took your father."

Michiko ran to her mother. "You said my father was working in the mountains," she said, searching her mother's face.

"He *is* working in the mountains," her mother replied

tiredly as she smoothed the top of her daughter's head. "He is building a road and receiving a wage." But her voice sounded strange, as if she was unsure of what she was saying.

Michiko turned to her aunt. "Is that true?"

Sadie shrugged. "You can call it work and wages if you like, Eiko." She walked over to the wooden box beside the stove. "You should start reading the newspaper, my little Japanese princess." Sadie bent down and removed several logs. "That is, if you can find it." She pulled out a newspaper, dusted it off and handed it to Michiko. "Soon you won't be the only Dirty Jap vacationing in this town."

Ted crossed the room in two strides and snatched the newspaper from Sadie's hand. He opened the iron grate of the big black stove and threw it into the fire. It went up in a blaze.

"That won't change anything!" Sadie yelled. Then she slumped into the chair and put her head in her hands. "That won't change anything," she mumbled.

Ted sat opposite her. "You are right." He took one of her hands and held it. "We can't change anything, but we can be brave."

Sadie didn't look up. The only sound in the kitchen was the hissing of the kettle.

After a short while, Ted let go of her hand. He picked up Hiro, went to the door and lifted the lantern from its nail. "I was going to wait until tomorrow to show you something," he said. He jiggled Hiro up and down and stuck his hand out to Michiko. "But I think now is a good time for my surprise."

"We don't need any more surprises," Eiko protested. "It's dark, and dinner is ready."

"It won't take long, I promise," Ted said as he stood at the door, holding Hiro. "I want all of you to come." His voice softened. "Sadie."

Michiko grabbed her uncle's hand.

"Sadie," Ted said, "you like surprises better than anyone."

"What about Geechan?" Michiko asked. Her grandfather wasn't in the house.

"He's known about it all along," Ted said. "In fact, he's there right now."

Ted led the family to the apple depot. The thick black outlines of pine trees hovered over them. The river seemed noisier. From the distance came the lonely whistle of the passing train.

"Don't push the doors all the way open," Ted cautioned them when they arrived.

One by one, they slid inside. The building smelled strongly of freshly sawn wood. Brown winged moths circled the lone electric light bulb overhead. Geechan stood next to a huge hump of canvas on carpenter trestles.

"It's not finished yet," Ted said, pulling the canvas back.

Sadie gasped. Then she shrieked. "It's a boat!" She ran her fingers across the wood. "How have you managed this?"

"The government directed us to burn the excess wood," Ted told her. "That seemed such a waste." He ran his fingers along the ribs. "We made the jig from the stuff lying about this place."

Michiko walked around the upside down hull. "How do you know how to do this?"

Her mother spoke for the first time. "It's like making a dress. You put the shape that you want at both ends and in the middle. Then you sew them together with wood."

Ted laughed. "That's right." He passed Hiro to Sadie. "Now that the frame is done," he said, "there are only two more things to do." He walked to the drawstring bag hanging from a nail on a post. Tacked above it was a photograph of a Japanese-style fishing sampan. Ted reached into the bag. "I'll use this," he said as he pulled out a wooden-handled plane. "The most important tool of all," he said, caressing the handle. "I'll use this to shave the wood as smooth as Hiro's cheek."

"You make it sound so easy," Eiko said.

"It's easy," Ted replied, "when you love your work."

Sadie turned to Geechan. "What was that old saying?" she asked. "One tenth of a boat builder's pay is for doing the job."

"And the rest is for knowing how to do it," Eiko finished for her.

"Can I help?" Michiko ran to her uncle. "Can I help you build your boat?"

"You can help me paint it," Ted said, placing his hand on her head. "Then we can think of a name."

Michiko looked around and thought for a moment. "Why don't you call it the *Apple?*"

Ted picked her up. "Perfect," he said. He twirled her about. "We'll paint it red. We'll call our little red rowboat the *Apple.*" He looked at Sadie and Eiko. "Fall down seven times, get up eight."

Ten

Carpenter Creek

Just after dawn, Michiko and Uncle Ted followed the thin dirt trail that led to the river. The tall grass and leaves felt wet. "It's good to be up early," he told her as she stifled a yawn. "We want fish that are looking for their breakfast."

A loud smack made Michiko freeze in fear of what might happen next. She looked at her uncle and whispered, "What was that?"

"A tail slap," her uncle replied. "When beavers sense danger, they whack their tails hard." He laughed. "First time I heard it, I didn't know what it was either."

"Look," he said, pointing to the sharpened stub of a stump. "It's been freshly cut." Beside it, in a pile of chips, lay the trunk of a giant cottonwood. "They must be close by."

"Are beavers dangerous?" asked Michiko.

"No, they will hide until we pass," he said. "They know human smell."

"Why did they chew down a whole tree?"

"They have to get at the leaves for food," he answered. "Then they use the rest for their home."

"Can we look for their home?" Michiko glanced

along the bank, picturing a small log cabin with a round door and smoking chimney.

"We'll probably pass it in the boat," Ted said.

They stepped through a patch of bushes, to the water, as the morning breeze pushed the clouds down river. The small beach of firm, damp sand sparkled like a glazed mud pie.

Jutting sideways from the bank was a giant, mottled trunk. The *Apple* nodded under an archway of bent willow branches. Ted walked along the trunk and tossed his tackle box and rods into the boat. Then he returned and took the *furoshiki* from Michiko.

She clutched his hand as she climbed onto the trunk. The branches swayed in the muddy water. She didn't like this part. What if she slipped into the cold water below?

The croak of an old bullfrog and the chip, chip, chipping sound of a red-winged blackbird drifted across the water. Soon they were gliding past wooden shores strewn with bluebells. Lush grass flanking the banks waved in the breeze, and cedars whispered as they floated by. Michiko trailed her hand in the clear, cold mountain water. She could see right to the bottom. The sparkle of the sun on the ripples made her dreamy.

"Look," Ted whispered. "There's where the beavers live." He pointed to the small stream that led away from the river.

Michiko scanned the water. "I can't see any house," she said, cupping her hand over her eyes. All she could see was a large muddy mound of sticks and branches.

"They live behind that bridge of branches," Ted told her.

"Where is the door?" she asked. "How do they get in and out?"

"They dive in the water and come up through a door in the floor of their house."

"Like a secret passage?"

"Just like a secret passage," he said with a nod.

A sudden sharp whistle startled them both. Clarence, standing on the grassy bank, waved. "Hey, Millie," he called out. Then he cupped his hands to his mouth and yelled, "Catch anything?"

"What is that boy saying?" Ted asked.

"He's from my school," Michiko told him. She ignored the fact that he had called her Millie. "He wants to know if we caught anything."

Ted rowed to where the green turf sloped down to the edge and whistled in answer.

There was a rustle, and Clarence's flaming red head peered down at them. "Nice boat," he called down, "my favourite colour." His face broke into a wide grin.

"Clarence," Michiko said politely, "I'd like you to meet my Uncle Ted."

Clarence saluted, and the string hanging from the end of the long stick he carried over his shoulder bounced. Michiko spotted a half-opened safety pin and a red and white wooden bobber dangling at his knees.

"You know any good fishing spots?" Ted asked.

"There's a place not far downstream," Clarence told them. He pointed with his rod and said, "Plenty of birds around."

"Where there are birds, there's fish," Ted responded.

"Do you want to come along?"

"Sure," responded Clarence enthusiastically. He scrambled down the side, balanced on a thick root and stepped in.

As the morning sun moved west, they spotted a pair of loons and a great blue heron. Ted replaced Clarence's safety pin with a hook and showed him how to swing his rod high across his shoulder, then with a snapping stroke, whip it downward. The string shot out and drifted on the water.

Ted put a worm on Michiko's hook and cast out her line for her. As she watched minnows shimmer in the water, her thoughts drifted to her goldfish. She hoped he was still Happy, living with the people next door.

Suddenly the water swelled, and a gaping mouth broke through the surface. The dragonfly hovering before her eyes disappeared. Michiko raised her head in surprise. Her bobber dipped below the water. She tugged at the rod, but nothing tugged back. When she reeled it in, the worm was gone.

"Let's try a minnow," Ted suggested. Michiko closed her eyes as he squished one onto the end of her hook. She lowered it slowly into the water.

Once again, the bobber dipped. Michiko tugged, and her rod bent. The reel screeched as she pulled the line toward her, and the rod nearly flew from her hands. "Help," she cried out.

"Keep the rod up," Clarence yelled.

"Stand up and plant your feet," Ted told her.

Michiko rose as Ted grabbed her by the seat of her

overalls. The trout put up a tremendous fight, leaping and twisting, but could not break the line. Finally, when it could fight no more, Ted took the rod and reeled it in. The pink and black speckled trout barely fit into the net.

"What a beauty," Clarence said with admiration.

"That's a mighty big fish for your very first time," Ted added.

"It made me tired," Michiko said, sinking down into the boat, "and sad."

"Don't be sad," Ted advised. "Just think of all that nice pink meat on your plate."

"My ma would be real pleased with that one," Clarence said with a smile. "That's enough fish for a family feast."

"How many are there in your family?" Ted asked.

"Five, when Dad's home."

"Is your dad at war?" asked Michiko.

"Naw," Clarence replied. "He's a railroad man. He walks the tracks."

"I think it time for lunch," said Ted as he maneuvered the boat to the side of the creek. As he moored it to a rock, he gave a long, low whistle. Then he beckoned them to his end of the rowboat and pointed.

Michiko's eyes followed his finger. On the side of the rock were several red-brown line drawings. One of them was the shape of a sun. Several looked like arrows. There were a few zigzags.

"Do you know what these are?" her uncle asked in a hushed tone.

"It looks like someone was drawing on the rocks with their crayons," Michiko suggested.

"Crayons would have washed away," Ted said. "I think these are petroglyphs, you know, rock paintings."

"Who made them?"

"Could have been Kootenays," Clarence said. "Our teacher told us the Kootenay Indians were sometimes called People of the Standing Arrow." His finger traced the outlines.

"These must be really old," Ted said, "Kootenays aren't around any more."

"What happened to them?" asked Michiko.

"Who knows?" Ted responded with a shrug, "Probably the same thing that happened to all Indian tribes, even those in Japan."

"Indians in Japan?" Clarence repeated it as if he hadn't heard correctly the first time. He sat in the bow of the boat gaping.

"The Ainu tribe," Ted said, untying the bundle of cloth that held their lunch, "still lives in Japan."

"Do they do Indian stuff?" Clarence asked.

"Depends what you mean by Indian stuff."

"Do they hunt and fish and build teepees?" Michiko asked.

"They build houses like teepees," Ted replied as he tossed Clarence a rice ball. "They put up three big branches and weave walls of bamboo grass."

Clarence turned the rice ball around, examining it. Then he popped it into his mouth. His eyes grew wide. "Good," he mumbled.

Michiko held her rice ball on the palm of her hand and nibbled it.

"Did the Ainu draw rock pictures too?" she asked.

Ted shrugged. "I don't know," he said. "All I know is the bear is important to them." He tossed Clarence a second rice ball. "You know something funny?" he asked.

"What," they said in unison. Michiko giggled.

"Both tribes, on different sides of the world, knew the same things." He patted the side of the red rowboat. "They both knew how to build boats and how to catch fish."

They finished their lunch in silence. Michiko thought about the people of the wilderness.

"Well, Clarence," Ted said when everything they'd brought was eaten. "You and I have got to do some serious fishing." He pushed the *Apple* away from shore and let it drift.

Clarence stuck a fresh minnow on his hook and threw his line over the side.

By the time the sun went behind the mountains, a dozen shimmering trout flopped about the bottom of the boat.

"Thanks a lot," Clarence said to Ted as they returned the small red boat to its wooded cove. He held his fish up with pride as he made his way into the forest. Then he stopped, turned back and yelled. "See you in school, Millie."

Michiko looked sideways at her uncle. Busy with his tackle box, he didn't seem to have noticed.

Eleven
How to Spot a Jap

The next morning, Michiko found Clarence waiting for her by the bridge. They leaned over the railing, watching the river rush noisily around the bend. Michiko pondered the differences between them. She wondered if Clarence knew she was Japanese. Together they walked up the main road to the schoolyard.

George's bike rested against the school wall. He stood on top of the schoolyard picnic table, waving a roll of yellow paper. "I'm telling you," he said as he hit his knee with the paper, "soon this place will be swarming with them."

Clarence leaned his tall, thin frame against the side wall. Michiko moved into the shade of the only tree in the dusty yard. Even though it was early, the sun beat down without mercy.

"Those houses in the orchard are being built for Japs," George announced.

"Why?" asked a boy from the crowd.

"Because they got kicked off the Island," George replied. "Don't you know there's a war going on?"

"My dad's gone off to fight," another boy announced proudly.

"Bob's dad is off fighting the Japs," George said. "What do we do?"

No one spoke, making George answer his own question. "We build houses and make them feel right at home." He pointed the roll of paper at the crowd. "Is that fair?" he asked. "Is it fair that Bob's dad is fighting the Japs, and we're helping them?"

The children looked at each other. A couple of them shrugged.

Then one boy spoke up. "I thought the new people in town were Chinese."

"I'm telling you they're Japs," George said.

"How are we supposed to know the difference?" a girl asked.

Michiko wrapped her arms around her waist, her stomach in knots.

George waved the roll of paper in his hands with glee. "I was hoping you'd ask," he said. He smacked it into the palm of his hand. "This is what I want to show you." He turned the roll sideways and opened it. "My dad brought this home from the city."

The crowd of boys and girls surged forward.

"Two men are picked up by a patrol," George read out loudly.

"What's a patrol?" one of the girls asked.

"It's a military word," George barked. "Stop interrupting." He began again. *"Two men are picked up by a patrol. One man is Chinese, and one man is Japanese. How do you tell the difference?"* He stopped and eyed the crowd.

"Who cares?" Clarence called out loudly.

Everyone turned to see who had spoken.

"We all care," George retorted. "We don't want a bunch of Japanese here."

"Maybe they don't want to be here," Clarence remarked. "Did you think about that?"

"Maybe they need to go back to Japan," one of the boys offered.

"Maybe they're Canadians," Clarence said. "Maybe like most of us, their parents were born in another country, not them."

"Shut up, Clarence," George warned. "Just because your parents are from Ireland doesn't make everyone else's parents foreign."

Michiko looked down at the bundle in her hand. Today she had brought chopsticks. No one else would have chopsticks. How could she use them now? She felt ill.

Michiko moved out from under the tree and headed toward the road.

George spotted her leaving. "Hey, Millie," he called. "Where you going? Are you going back to one of those little houses in the orchard?"

Michiko stopped walking. She could feel every pair of eyes on her back.

Clarence walked up to George and snatched the pamphlet out of his hand.

"You know, George," he said with a smirk, "you're not as smart as you think you are." He stuffed the roll of paper into his back pocket. "Millie lives at the old Nelson place."

The crowd looked first at Michiko then at George.

Clarence spoke again. "Yesterday, Millie and I went

fishing on the Carpenter." He hooted. "She caught a fish bigger than anything you ever caught." He scuffed at the dirt with the toe of his boot and looked up. "How are you going to know the difference between Japanese and Chinese, when you can't even recognize a Kootenay Indian?"

The whole crowd erupted into laughter, just as Miss Henderson came out. She smiled at the scene of the children enjoying a good joke and rang the school bell. They all moved into line.

Clarence beckoned Michiko back with a nod of his head. The heat of the summer filled the classroom. He took his seat in front of Michiko and stashed the roll of yellow paper in his desk.

George glared at her. "So what's the name of your tribe?" he asked.

"My tribe?" she repeated.

"Yeah," he snarled, "your tribe." He raised his palm to the back of his head and waved his fingers. "If you have Indian blood," he said searching her face, "you should know the name of your tribe."

Michiko thought for a minute then whispered, "I come from a long line of people that hunt and fish." She lifted her head and raised her voice. "My people know the importance of boats." She thought about George's silver bicycle leaning against the brick wall, shining in the sun and continued: "We know boats are more much more important than bicycles."

"Boats will never be more important than bicycles," George said loudly.

Miss Henderson looked up from her desk and

rapped the side of it with her wooden ruler. George stopped talking.

Michiko crossed her arms and laid her head on top of them. How could this boy think that she was his enemy just because she was Japanese?

Over her arms, she saw the roll of yellow paper stuffed in Clarence's desk was within easy reach. Michiko formed a plan. As soon as the class stood for "God Save the King", she knocked her books to the floor. When she crouched to retrieve them, Michiko pulled the roll from Clarence's desk. She stuffed it deep into the pocket of her sundress.

Twelve
The Root Cellar

W e need to move this piece of linoleum," insisted Michiko's mother. "I can't sweep the floor properly."

"I'll hold up the corners," said Sadie. "Just sweep underneath. We don't have to move the whole thing."

"I need to do a proper job," Eiko argued.

"You better give us a hand," Sadie called to Michiko. "You know how fussy your mother is about cleaning."

Michiko helped tug the big black linoleum square across the room.

"It looks better over here, actually," said Sadie.

Michiko, like her aunt, surveyed the room. The Singer treadle machine stood under the window, a long narrow table beside it. Ted had built it especially for sewing. He had nailed a wooden yardstick along one edge and small wooden boxes for pins and buttons along another. Folded neatly at one end was her mother's futon. Once again, several of the gold rectangular patches of the quilt were in need of repair.

Geechan had repaired one of Mrs. Morrison's old rocking chairs. He had painted it blue, the same colour as the kitchen chairs. Now everything matched. They even had a vase for flowers on top of an oilcloth. Mrs. Morrison had brought them one day to replace the jam jar.

There were curtains on the windows, shelves along the walls and benches below.

Outside Ted had attached a woodshed to the kitchen to keep the wood dry. A wall of kindling waited inside. There was even a rain barrel at the end of the verandah to collect water for washing their hair.

Everyone worked hard at making the farmhouse home, Michiko thought. She felt good when she thought about it.

When Michiko's mother turned to retrieve the broom, she gasped. Sadie and Michiko followed her gaze, and they gasped as well.

In the middle of the kitchen floor was a small, square wooden door. A black iron ring fit into a carved wooden pocket. The door and the handle were flush with the floor.

"It's like the secret passage to a beaver's house," Michiko squealed in delight. She was the first to kneel beside it.

"Ahh," murmured Sadie, "this must lead to the lost gold mines of the Aztecs."

"There weren't any Aztecs around here," Michiko said.

"Ahh," Sadie continued, "but there were plenty of silver mines." She lifted the handle and gave it a tug. It wouldn't open.

Everyone tried, but the door wouldn't budge.

"We will have to wait until Ted comes," Michiko's mother said. "Maybe he can jimmy it with a tool."

A knock on the door made them all look up. "Only me," called out Mrs. Morrison as she let herself in.

"Looks like you've found the root cellar," she remarked, seeing the door in the floor.

"What's a root cellar?" Michiko asked. She imagined a huge network of roots below, forming passages and tunnels that she and Clarence could explore.

"It's an underground pantry," Mrs. Morrison explained. "Mine is built into the side of a small hill." She plodded to the door in the floor. "I don't use it any more," she confessed. "I've got a refrigerator."

She planted her thick legs on either side of the door. She bent down. "There's a knack to opening these things," she said. She gave the handle a bit of a jiggle. She turned it to the left and listened. "That's it," she said and gave the door a heave. It opened with a cloud of dust.

Puffing from the exertion, Mrs. Morrison placed one hand on her chest and staggered backwards into the rocking chair. "Look under the door," she wheezed and pointed. "There should be a support stake. Pull it down."

Sadie pulled a lever out of a slat. She propped up the door. The dank smell of rotten potatoes filled the kitchen. Michiko leaned over the gaping hole. "It's really dark down there."

"Get the lantern," Mrs. Morrison ordered.

Eiko took the lantern down from the wall. She lit it and handed it to Sadie. Sadie held it in front of her as she descended the short ladder.

Mrs. Morrison rose from her chair and headed out the front door.

"It can't be time for you to leave," Michiko's mother called out after her. "You haven't had your tea."

"I'm not going far," said the voice on the verandah. "That's the winter entrance. There has got to be a summer one."

Michiko dashed out behind her.

She watched Mrs. Morrison poke along the side of the house with a stick. Suddenly she threw down the stick. She leaned against the side of the house. "That will be it," she said with great satisfaction. "Give that grass a good tug, young lady."

Michiko tugged. A large piece of turf came away, revealing a dirty grey plank. Michiko brushed the dirt from her hands. "That will be the summer entrance," Mrs. Morrison informed her, "once it's cleared away."

Using the stick as a cane, she stomped up the stairs. "It's a short season in these parts," she said. "A few potatoes and onions in that root cellar will get you through the long winter. You need to put in a garden."

Michiko looked at the long grass surrounding the house. "How big a garden?" she asked. "Where would we get seeds?"

"At the general store." Mrs. Morrison said. "But," she paused to catch her breath, "you can get any kind of seeds you want from a Seed Catalogue."

Mrs. Morrison sank into the rocking chair. "The Seed Catalogue arrives every spring." She paused. Michiko listened to the sound of the wooden rockers squeaking against the linoleum. "When I was young," Mrs. Morrison chuckled, "I didn't know any of those fancy Latin names for plants," she continued. "I wanted to order something special." She chuckled again. "I ordered a package of seeds for a plant called lovage."

"Did the lovage grow?" Michiko asked.

"Huge bushes of green leaves came up along the wooden gate. The leaves were forked and spiky."

"Were there flowers?"

"The bushes eventually flowered. They had tiny yellow knobby flowers."

"Did they have any perfume?"

"Oh, there was a smell about them," she said, "but it wasn't perfume."

"What did it smell like?"

"Celery," she said. Mrs. Morrison threw back her head and laughed. "My whole flower garden smelled like celery."

"What did your mother think?"

"She wasn't happy," the woman replied. "She thought that I'd completely wasted my money." She leaned into Michiko's face. "But the German woman at the next farm was very happy."

"Why?"

"In Germany, lovage is used in potato dishes." Mrs. Morrison laughed again and slapped her knee. "She picked it by the handfuls and gave my mother a great big lump of cheese in exchange. That made my mother happy. But, after that, I only ordered seeds for plants I knew."

Suddenly Mrs. Morrison changed the subject. "You don't take the newspaper," she asked Michiko's mother, "do you?"

"Sadie picks it up on occasion," Eiko responded. "I wish she wouldn't," she mumbled.

"I cut something out," Mrs. Morrison said, fumbling in her large purse. She produced a folded piece of newsprint and placed it on the table. Then after taking a sip of tea, she proceeded to read.

"If you are going to do canning this season, be sure to get a Canning Guide from the Post Office." She took another sip of her tea.

"I guess it would be a good idea," Eiko mused.

Mrs. Morrison continued. *"Fill out the Application for Canning Sugar in the Number Two Ration Book. Fill in your application as a housewife for all members of your household on your own card. State the number of persons for whom you are applying, but not including yourself. The blank cards of each member of your household should be attached to your card. Forward them to your Local Ration Board."*

"I don't know if it's worth all the trouble," Eiko said. "We don't have the necessary supplies. We need jars, a boiling pot and wax for the tops. Where will I get all that?"

"I've got most of it." Mrs. Morrison slapped her hand down on the table. "You get the sugar, I'll provide the equipment." She looked up at the ceiling and smiled. "I just love making preserves."

Michiko's mother smiled too. "What are we going to preserve?"

"Huckleberries," Mrs. Morrison responded. "There will be more huckleberries in these parts than you have ever seen."

"Huckleberries," Michiko's mother repeated.

At the sound of the truck horn, Mrs. Morrison

heaved herself from the chair. "I can almost taste huckleberry jam." She stood for a moment to catch her breath. "Head on down with that baby carriage, and we'll fill it up with jars." She stomped towards the door. "Lovage," she muttered and chuckled. "I haven't thought about lovage in years."

In the weeks that followed, all Michiko could think about was planting. She would plant flowers all around the verandah. She would plant scarlet snapdragons and white lilies.

Thirteen
Mail Order Catalogues

Michiko accompanied her aunt and uncle into town. They passed the church, the bank and the school, following along the wooden sidewalk.

Boards covered most of windows of the buildings near the train station. The walkway across the tracks was in need of repair. The General Store still operated, even though the Hardware Store next to it had closed down.

Across from the station house was the town's only hotel. Lines of drying clothes filled the dilapidated balconies. Several Japanese children played on the large wooden steps. Some played baseball in the vacant lot next door.

Michiko, Ted and Sadie entered the large weatherbeaten building of the General Store. It was warm inside and smelled of old paper and wood. A long wooden counter extended across the entire back wall. To one side was a wicket. Behind it, a tall, bony woman in a navy dress with a starched lace collar waited on a customer. A couple waited their turn. They glanced up and turned their backs on Michiko, her aunt and uncle.

"We have to have the right coupons," Sadie said,

stopping to fish through her purse. "As if finding the money isn't enough." She pulled out a sheet of perforated stamps and handed it to Michiko.

Michiko bent the first row over along the perforation.

"No!" exclaimed her aunt. "We have to tear them off in front of the store clerk." She took the page back. "We have to make sure we follow the rules."

Michiko's eyes widened. If anyone was famous for breaking rules, it was Sadie.

Michiko wandered down the aisles. She examined the contents of the shelves in the first aisle, reading the labels aloud. The bright red boxes of soda crackers caught her eye. She remembered having them in her cupboard at home. Below them was a small assortment of canned goods. She looked for canned peaches, her favourite. Then she stopped suddenly. Tacked to the shelf was a small hand-printed sign. *"When the Japs give in,"* was the first line; *"We'll have more tin,"* was the second.

Michiko looked around. She removed the thumbtack, folded the cardboard in half and slipped it into her coat pocket. She stuck the thumbtack back into the wood.

The bell over the door jingled, giving Michiko a start. She walked to the top of the aisle.

The postmistress handed the woman a brown box tied with string. "Looks like your daughter's winter boots have arrived," she said. Her scrawny neck throbbed like a lizard.

"She'll be pleased," the woman responded. "I ordered the white ones with fur trim."

The postmistress nodded in approval. Then looking past Ted, she spoke to the woman who had just come in. "May I help you?"

Ted coughed.

The woman spoke up. "I believe this gentleman was ahead of me."

The postmistress sniffed and held her fingers to her throat as she turned to Ted. "Name and address, please," she asked, her voice full of vinegar.

Ted gave her the information. She examined the contents of one of the cubby holes behind her, pulled out a thin brown envelope and slid it through the space below the wicket.

"Thank you," Ted said. The postmistress looked past him. Ted did not move away from the wicket. "I need three stamps as well," he told her and slapped his money on the counter.

Michiko moved to where Sadie was completing her purchases. The woman helping her was smiling pleasantly.

"Can I help you too?" she asked Michiko.

"I want to buy some seeds," Michiko said.

"The planting season is over," the woman responded. "All of our packets are sold."

"I just wanted to plant some flowers," Michiko said.

"Ahh, I see." The woman said. She reached beneath the counter and pulled out a small catalogue. She pushed it towards Michiko. "You can order them," she explained.

Michiko pulled the catalogue towards her. "Thanks," she said quietly.

"Wait a minute," the woman told her. "There will be

other things you'll need." She looked at Michiko and winked. "If it's a big garden, you may need a tractor."

Michiko looked up at Sadie in surprise. Her aunt gave a wide grin.

The woman returned with a second catalogue. This one was much thicker. A broad band of brown paper kept it taut. "I don't know a girl who doesn't enjoy the Eaton's catalogue."

That night, Michiko sat down at the kitchen table to investigate her catalogues. Something crackled in her pocket. Michiko pulled out the sign from the store and read it again. She creased the cardboard along the fold. Then she tore it. She folded it and tore it again. She kept on folding and tearing until it was a handful of ragged confetti. Then she threw the pieces onto the fire.

She opened the seed catalogue and glanced through the flower section. There were daisies, sweet William, and yarrow. There weren't any snapdragons or lilies. It looked as if her plan to surprise her mother wouldn't be possible.

Michiko flipped through a selection of peas. Imagine planting peas with the name "Content", she thought. She shoved the seed catalogue aside. She broke the brown paper seal and opened the second catalogue.

The first thing she recognized was the upright-style table toaster they'd used at home.

She looked at the picture of a young woman modelling a dress. It had square shoulders and a smatter of glittering sequins across the neckline. *This is Aunt Sadie's kind of dress*, Michiko thought. Then she corrected herself. "This is the kind of dress she used to wear." Gone were her aunt's bright red lipstick and her delicate flower smell.

Her eyes fell on the picture of the silver bracelet with five small bells. Beside it, there was a bracelet with a four-leaf clover, a musical note and a star. "And who isn't wearing bracelets by the armful these days?" was written below. "I'm not," Michiko said aloud.

A pearl necklace with a filigree clasp made her think of her mother's tears.

Michiko flipped to another section. There was a dollhouse with a removable roof and a family of dolls. She read the description of the drumming bear. "Wind his key, and his head moves side to side. Both arms beat the drum vigorously." *Just like my toy monkey. The one I had to leave behind.* She closed her eyes. Michiko remembered the toys on her bedroom shelf at home. She remembered her birthday presents. Then she turned the page.

Princess Minnehaha was ten and a half inches tall. She wore a beaded tunic, and sticking out of her bandeau was a small feather. For only one dollar, Michiko could buy the very person she was pretending to be.

In bed that night, Michiko listened to the household sounds that were now part of her life. She heard the clank of the aluminum kettle and the hiss of water dropping on the hot iron plate. Michiko closed her eyes to the thud of a log dropping in the great iron stove. A terrible heaviness formed around her heart. The sound of an owl screeching in the forest added to the awful feeling growing in her heart. She was beginning to think they would never be going back.

Fourteen

Bears

"O uch," Michiko complained. "You're pulling too tight."

"I'm almost done," her aunt said. "Sit still. Once it's braided, you can sit in the sun and let it dry."

Sadie stood back to study her handiwork. She lifted the ends of the two braids and sat them on top of her niece's head. "Maybe we should cut them off," she suggested.

Michiko stared up at her aunt in horror. "My braids?" she wailed. Both hands flew to the top of her head.

"Shall I?"

"No," she stated firmly. "Father wouldn't like that."

"I'm sure he would still recognize you," Sadie said with a smile.

Michiko had wondered about cutting her braids, but they were an important part of her secret identity. None of the other children at school seemed to care if she was Japanese, but it mattered to George. His dislike of Japanese people was intense, and he wasn't ashamed to let people know it.

Every now and then, she stuck a feather in one of her braids to make Clarence laugh.

After the fishing trip, she and Clarence had become friends. Sometimes they searched for gold nuggets along the creek bed. Even though the mountain water was ice cold, Clarence panned in it, believing, one day, it would bring them gold.

Michiko taught Clarence how to make paper boats. They used the pages from George's pamphlet and launched the Yellow Belly Fleet. They pretended each boat would return with a nugget of gold on board.

One afternoon they lay on their backs in the orchard munching early apples. They watched the sky. All about them was the humming of lazy bees.

"Look," Michiko said, pointing to a fat rolling cloud, "that's the shape of a peach."

"I hate peaches," Clarence said.

"How can you hate peaches?" Michiko asked in surprise.

"You don't know?" he responded. Clarence tugged at a golden red curl. "George calls me Peach Boy all the time."

Clarence's hair and pale skin reminded Michiko of a peach as well.

"That's a compliment," she told him.

"How can it be a compliment?" Clarence complained as he rolled over on to his stomach.

That day, Michiko had told Clarence the story of Momo-Taro, the boy born from a peach.

Michiko shook her braids now and stopped daydreaming. "I've got to get going," she told her aunt. "I'm meeting Clarence. We're picking blueberries."

Bert was taking a load of pickers up to the mountains. For each pail picked and delivered, he credited them with twenty-five cents, which he recorded in his little black book. Clarence had told her that at the end of the picking season last year, he had amassed the small fortune of five dollars. Instead of having them walk five miles to his farm, Mrs. Morrison had persuaded Bert to pick them up at the bridge.

There was no sign of Clarence when Michiko arrived, but she knew he would emerge suddenly from one of the fields. Michiko thought he was brave to walk the tracks. It frightened her to hear he walked the trestle that spanned the creek.

"Aren't you worried about a train coming?" she'd asked.

"Nah," he'd scoffed. "My old man's a railway man. I know all the schedules."

The familiar green pick-up truck turned the corner and rumbled across the wooden planks. Bert steered with one hand while the other dangled out of the window. "Get in the back," he barked as he stopped. Several Japanese women wearing floppy hats tied under the chin stared at her. Their fingers showed through holes cut in lengths of old socks.

Michiko didn't join them. She looked up and down the road.

"I ain't waiting around all day," Bert snapped. "You coming or not?"

There was no sign of Clarence. Michiko was in no hurry to experience another ride hanging on to loose, rattling boards. Besides, she wouldn't go without Clarence. She shook her head.

Bert snorted and drove off.

Michiko decided Clarence must have forgotten and headed back home.

When she reached the orchard, someone came running full pelt down the lane. Michiko lifted her hand to shield her eyes from the sun. The sun caught the runner's bright red hair. Why was Clarence coming from this direction?

He arrived, panting. He wrapped his arms about his waist and bent over.

"The truck already left," Michiko told him. "Didn't you see it go by?"

"Bears," was the only word he could get out. He put both hands on his knees and breathed in deeply.

"What did you say?"

Clarence pointed down the road. "Bears," he repeated. He continued to pant. "I came out of the field and almost fell over them. They were in the ditch."

"Real bears?"

Clarence nodded. "They don't usually come this close to town." His face was bright red.

"What are they doing?"

"They're feeding off those berry bushes by the road." Finally he stood up straight. "I had to back away and run along the tracks."

"Take me to see them," Michiko pleaded. "I've only seen bears in the zoo."

"You'll have to be real quiet," Clarence warned. "You don't mess with bears."

They walked down the road in silence. Suddenly Clarence stopped and stuck out his arm to prevent her from going further. Two young bears wrestled in the tall grass at the verge of a small hill. One wore a magnificent honey blonde coat. It had a dark face and dark ears. The other was plain brown. They stopped rolling and batted at the shrubbery about them using their clawed paws. "Don't make any sudden movements," Clarence cautioned. He took her arm and pulled her to an outcrop of quartz. "Let's get behind these rocks."

The bushes drooped with berries. Michiko could see their little pink tongues dart in and out as they tasted the dark fruit. *Would her tongue turn blue like theirs had?*

Then the brown one turned his attention to a rock. He used his paw to heave it out of the ground. He nosed about the hollow.

"What are you two doing?" came a voice from behind them. It was George. Michiko and Clarence were so engrossed that he had ridden up unheard.

Clarence put a finger to his lip. "Sshh," he whispered. "We're bear-watching."

George stood beside his bike. He looked across the road. "They're just a couple of cubs," he scoffed.

"Babies are never far from their mothers," Michiko told him. She was thinking of Hiro.

"She's right," said Clarence. "I wouldn't argue with a Kootenay. They know all about bears." He winked.

Just then a large silvertip grizzly ambled out of the trees, and the three of them gasped. George lowered his bike and got behind the rock.

The cubs must have picked up his scent. They looked to their mother, but she paid no attention. They moved out of the ditch closer to her. The mother bear touched noses with one of the cubs. The other tried to climb onto her back.

"Hey, look," said George as he pointed at the two figures emerging from the forest.

Michiko peered over the rock. She recognized them at once. One was Tadoshi, the old carpenter who worked with her Uncle Ted. The other was Geechan. They had become fast friends and often walked and talked together.

The men approached the clump of berry bushes and stopped. The bears were behind the bushes in the meadow. *Turn back,* Michiko wished desperately, *turn back.*

"They're Japs," George remarked.

"How do you know that?" Clarence asked.

"Look at their skin," he whispered. "It's like a lemon colour." He rubbed his hands in glee. "Wait until they get closer," he said. "You'll see how their eyes slant towards their nose. If they scream, we'll get to see their big buck teeth."

Michiko looked at George in surprise.

"Too bad they got shoes on," George commented. "If they had their wooden sandals, we could see their six toes."

Michiko emitted a short involuntary shriek that sounded like hysterical laughter. She couldn't help it. What George had just said was absolutely ridiculous.

George looked at her approvingly. "Yeah," he said with a smirk. "We'll get a good laugh when those two old Jap men meet up with those bears." He patted her on the back, but his touch made her shudder.

Geechan and Tadoshi remained standing. They were engrossed in each other's words. Then they each took a stance. It was as if they were acting out a *karate* match.

Suddenly, Clarence leaped up and jumped on to George's bike. Screaming *"Bonsai!"* he tore off down the road, yelling in what he hoped sounded like Japanese.

The big silver bear looked up. She bounded across the meadow, back into the woods, with her cubs behind. The two men stood and stared.

Clarence returned. "That was great," he said with satisfaction. "I scared them both." He leaned the bike against the boulder.

George stood up in anger. "You were supposed to let the bears scare the Japs," he growled at Clarence. "You don't know how to do anything right." He yanked his bike from the ground and rode off.

Clarence peered over the rock. "It's okay," he told Michiko. "The bears are gone."

She looked up at him, her eyes moist with tears. She picked up a rock and heaved it as hard as she could across the road. She was angry with George. Geechan and Tadoshi could have been hurt. But most of all, she was angry with herself. She had just pretended not to know her very own grandfather.

Fifteen
Camp School

It glowed so bright, Michiko had to squint to see out her window. She pressed her palm to the pane, and the lace of frost melted. Fine white crystals covered the entire world. Every branch of every tree sparkled. Tiny twigs twinkled like wands, and the pine tops wore tiaras. It was a world of gleaming ice. Michiko looked towards the mountains. The glittering surface stretched on endlessly into the sun.

She dressed quickly and raced to the kitchen. Pulling on her boots, she stepped outside. The ice crackled beneath her feet.

A set of footprints led down the steps. Geechan stood talking with one of the local farmers. Once a week, he sold them dry beans. Sometimes he brought freshly baked bread from his wife's kitchen.

The two men chatted beside the farmer's horse-drawn sled. Icicles hung from the ledge of the tiny windows of the little barnboard house on rails. The wooden boxes stacked about the flat roof were pillowed with snow. The sleek black horse wore several burlap sacks. His harness bells glistened with frost. The large bundled man gestured broadly with red, swollen hands wrapped in rags. He mimicked shooting a rifle.

Sadie knocked icicles from the edge of the roof with the broom handle. They clattered and smashed at her feet. "This way," she said, picking up the shards and putting them in a bucket, "we can save ourselves a trip to the creek."

"You'll turn into an icicle yourself without a coat," Eiko said at the doorway. Michiko followed Sadie inside.

Sadie placed the bucket on the stove. Michiko munched a piece of toast spread with sardines and watched the icicles lower themselves into their hot, steamy bath.

Geechan entered carrying a wooden box of supplies. "No school," he told his granddaughter. "Too slippery."

"I should think not," Sadie remarked. She smiled and said, "Unless you hitched a ride."

Geechan told them the farmer had shot a wolf. They were so hungry, they came out of the mountains to hunt farm animals. Sadie and Michiko looked at each other with wide eyes.

Wednesday was baking day. Michiko was glad she didn't have to go to school. She helped dry the dishes. Then she settled at the end of the small table to read.

Geechan sat at the other end peeling apples. Michiko and Clarence had picked every apple that grew on the trees at the side of the house. They had stored them between layers of pine needles in the root cellar.

The rough round apple turned slowly in Geechan's

dark, coarse hands. As the white flesh appeared, a ribbon of peel unwound downward. He laughed and held it up in the air for her to see. Then he jiggled it. For a single minute, it held the shape of the apple before collapsing on the oilcloth. Michiko smiled. Then he sliced the apple into thin wedges and ate them off the tip of his knife.

Her mother hummed as she worked bent over the stove. The oven door clanged open. She put her hand in and began to count aloud. "One, two, three," she said in a singsong voice. Michiko joined in, "twenty-three, twenty-four, twenty-five."

"Hot enough," her mother said and pulled out her hand. She placed a large sheet of round scones inside. The scones were for Mrs. Morrison.

Winter didn't stop Mrs. Morrison. She had unearthed a sleigh from her barn and put her farm horse in harness. The mare was short, stout and thick in the legs, just like her. Geechan rose to give her an apple for the horse.

Mrs. Morrison brought them all the news that flew about town. People were preparing for the winter. Drifting snow could make the ten miles of winding road to the next town impassable. The supplies on the store shelves were gone.

"Some snow banks are five feet high," she told them, struggling out of her shabby beaver coat. "The shovelled walks are only wide enough for one." Her large knuckles tugged at the knot in her woollen kerchief. "They are trying to decide where to put the new school."

"New school?" asked Michiko. "What's wrong with the old one?"

"Nothing, really," replied Mrs. Morrison. "There are so many children in town, they need to open another one."

"How will they decide which children go to which school?"

"Oh, that's easy," said Sadie. "The government has already made that decision." She banged the baking sheet. "The new school is for Japanese children only."

"Just Japanese children?" asked Michiko.

Michiko thought about the rows and rows of tiny houses with pencil-thin curls of smoke coming out of the chimneys. She and Clarence had visited the orchard to watch the older boys play baseball.

Kiko, one of the girls her age, had invited Michiko inside her house. It was a lot different from the way Michiko imagined. Tarpaper and cardboard patched the walls. Bedding was draped from the rafters, and clothes were hung from wooden pegs along the walls. The iron cook stove was half the size of the one they had. Kiko called it their *gangara* stove. There was no pump over a sink, just a galvanized tub and a bucket in the corner. They had to walk to the creek every day, even in the summer, for water. Two families occupied the house, sharing the kitchen.

"Do you mean to tell me the children have not gone to school yet at all?" Eiko asked.

"Believe it or not," said Mrs. Morrison, "they were holding classes out of doors." She split open a lightly browned scone. "There's a Japanese woman staying at the hotel." She smeared it with huckleberry preserves. "She's the supervisor setting up the school."

"Have you met her?" Michiko's mother asked. "What is she like?"

"All I know is she is looking for teachers," replied Mrs. Morrison.

Michiko thought about Miss Henderson. She was nice, but she didn't have much discipline. Some of the boys, especially George, often spoke out of turn.

"What about you, Auntie Sadie?" asked Michiko. All three women looked at her in surprise.

"What would I teach?" Sadie asked.

"English, Arithmetic, Art, Physical Education," Michiko said loudly, counting off her fingers. "Especially Music and Dance." Then she wagged a finger. "And they would listen to you."

"Maybe," Sadie mused as she took a sip of tea. "I could look into it."

"What are your plans for Christmas?" Mrs. Morrison suddenly asked.

"Christmas?" repeated Eiko.

Michiko looked up from her book. "What about Father?" She turned to her mother. "He has never missed a Christmas."

Sadie put her scone to one side. "I told you she would be asking soon."

Michiko threw her arms in the air and cried out. "What about my father?"

Her mother looked at Sadie. "I don't know," she said through tight lips. "I don't know when your father will be home." She put her head in her hands.

"You know, Michiko," Sadie said, "sometimes you

forget you are not the only one who misses him." She sat down next to her sister and put her arm around her shoulders.

"I'm sorry," said Michiko. She laid her head on her mother's back.

"You know something," Sadie said, "we could make some decorations. It would brighten the place up."

"I remember when I was a child," Mrs. Morrison mused. "We decorated the mantle with bows of greenery." She sighed. "We strung popcorn and hung cookies on the tree."

Michiko's mother gave a small smile. "There is no lack of pine around here," she said.

Michiko threw her hands up towards the ceiling and twirled around. "We can make paper chains." She danced over to Hiro. "We can do *origami*." She clapped her hands in front of her baby brother. "We can wrap presents." Then she stopped. "That is, if we had any."

The three women looked at each other and burst out laughing. They laughed so hard, tears streamed down their faces. Sadie and Eiko each used an end of the dishtowel to wipe their eyes. Mrs. Morrison pulled a laced handkerchief from her purse. Hiro grinned and gurgled.

Sadie stood up. "Well, that was good, thanks, Michiko." She pulled the kettle back onto the hot plate.

"Will you come?" Michiko asked Mrs. Morrison.

Mrs. Morrison put her teacup down. "Where?" She asked.

"Here, for Christmas?" Michiko explained. She looked into her mother's eyes. Her mother smiled.

"Yes," said Michiko's mother. "Please join us for Christmas."

Mrs. Morrison dabbed her eyes a second time. "I would love to," she said. She crumpled the lace into her large, moist hand. "But only under two conditions."

"Two conditions," Sadie repeated. "What would they be?"

Mrs. Morrison leaned forward as if to impart a great secret. "You must let me bring a turkey." Then she sat back suddenly and almost shouted, "My name is Edna." She put her hands on her hips and boomed, "You must all stop calling me Mrs. Morrison."

Sixteen

Winter Wolves

Michiko trudged home, watching the low grey clouds that hung in the sky. The only sound came from the crows. Perched along the bare branches, they squawked at each other with raspy throats. Her world had become nothing but black birds in grey trees.

Michiko used to like the tints of black and grey. She could remember an ink stone shaped like a lily pad used for preparing the ink-stick. The fine sable brush next to the roll of crisp white rice paper had given her the feeling of anticipation. Now, it was as if her whole world was *katakana,* long dark days stroking off the months.

A sudden blast of cold wind snatched her scarf from her neck. She grabbed on to the rim of her knitted hat and ran after it. Luckily, it had snagged on a tangle of branches. If she lost it, it would be a while before she got another.

Michiko's brown woollen coat was too tight. She wore several pairs of socks, but her feet were still cold. In bed, they were like two blocks of ice. Michiko thought she would never get warm all the way through again.

The worst was not having enough to eat. She

remembered a time when she used to leave rice in her bowl. Now, dinner was usually dried fiddleheads, cabbage and bacon. On her way home, Michiko recited the menu she really wanted. It was *miso* soup, *sunomono* salad, rice with red beans, *yakatori* and a large bottle of fizzy orange pop.

Poor Hiro, Michiko thought. *His first word was "more".*

The icy winds turned the road ruts to glass. The family's well had frozen. They had to haul their water for washing and cooking from the creek. Ted cut a hole in the ice where the current was swift enough to make the ice thin. He tied a rope to the tree and attached a long pole. They had to stir the water to prevent it from freezing over.

Michiko hated stirring with the stick. She hated dragging water up the slippery slope to the drums tied to the wooden sled. It sloshed everywhere. Sometimes the icy water splashed down her legs and inside her boots.

They heard stories of the women in the orchard sweeping the frost from their homes. The children's fingers stuck to the doorways. Snow piled up over their windows.

As she walked alongside the creek, Michiko thought about the frogs. She could picture them sleeping soundly under a lid of ice. Even they were warmer than Michiko and her family.

The branches of the bushes clacked, and the wind continued to blow. It began to rain. Michiko hunched down. Every muscle in her body ached. When she got to the front door, she barely had the strength to open it. She hit the door with her fist.

Geechan yanked it open and drew her in. He took her hands into his own and rubbed them hard. Her mother lit the coal oil lamp. Sadie put a large piece of wood into the stove, and her mother turned up the wick.

No one spoke.

The wind moaned its way through the branches of the apple trees. An icy blast shot under the door and across the room. Eiko rolled the rug which usually lay in front of the sink and stuffed it against the door. Sadie poured them all tea, and they sipped it together, sitting around the lantern.

Hiro slept peacefully in the carriage under the stairs.

The wind blew harder. The slow moan grew to a howl. Michiko thought about Clarence. He was so tall and thin. How would he manage to stand up against the wind?

The freezing rain pelted against the farmhouse like stones hitting the window.

Eiko got up to stir the large pot of soup on the stove. Geechan moved to the bench to whittle, and Sadie picked up a skein of yarn and began to knit.

The silence was profound as the storm lashed at the wooden farmhouse. The light bulb overhead sputtered and went out. The clicking needles stopped, and the room was full of shadows.

"I hope Ted's all right," Sadie said.

"Where is he?" Michiko asked.

"He left town to find work."

"How long will he be gone?" Michiko cried. She feared the men from the government. Was Ted on his way to the mountains as well?

"Who knows?" Sadie replied. The rain lashed against the window. She looked up. "By the looks of this weather, he won't be back soon."

After dinner, there wasn't much else for Michiko to do but go to bed. She climbed the stairs slowly. Lately she had been dreaming about her old bedroom. Couldn't they just go back for a short visit? Couldn't they go back and get some of their things?

Michiko undressed in the dark. The icy rain continued to clatter against the windows. She closed her eyes.

The sound of the farmhouse door banging in the middle of the night woke her. Hiro's crib stood black in the moonlight. She lifted her head and listened. Her baby brother breathed softly.

Suddenly, a wailing howl came from beneath her window. Michiko sat straight up in bed.

There was a scurry of footsteps in the hall. A door opened, then closed. Her mother tiptoed in. She rearranged Hiro's small blue blanket.

"Are you awake?' her mother asked soothingly. There was another howl. Eiko wrapped her arms about her daughter. Hiro stirred.

Sadie appeared in the doorway. "Father's not in his room," she said.

Michiko looked up at her mother. "I heard the door bang," she said. "He must have gone to the outhouse."

The three of them went downstairs. Michiko pulled on her coat and rubber boots. She opened the door, stepped carefully out on to the verandah and peeked around. A snowy white wolf stalked the small grey hut.

She could see its pointed ears and long tail clearly in the moonlight. She turned and ran inside.

"We need to open the summer door," Michiko said. "Geechan can run to the root cellar."

"It's probably frozen," Sadie said.

"We have to try," Michiko argued.

Sadie wrestled with the trap door while her mother lit the lantern. They descended into the cavern of chilled air. Michiko heard the scraping sound of the wooden bar coming off the door. She listened to them grunt and heave.

Sadie's head appeared in the opening of the floor. "Good thing he is thin," she said breathlessly. "We can open it enough, I think."

Michiko pulled out the large pail from under the sink. Then she took the kettle from the stove. She stepped out on to the verandah and sang her loudest. "*Sa-ku-ra,*" she sang as she clanged the pot and the kettle together. "*Sa-ku-ra,*" she screamed. She banged louder.

Hiro woke up and began to wail. *Good for you,* thought Michiko. *Make a lot of noise.*

The wolf backed into the orchard. Michiko knew she didn't dare go far from the door.

The door to the outhouse opened slightly. "Geechan," Michiko called out, "run to the root cellar." She banged the kettle against the pot again. She started to chant the words instead of singing them, "*Sa-ku-ra, Sa-ku-ra.*"

Hiro continued to howl.

Her mother appeared at her side. Using the broom, she knocked icicles from the roof. They clattered and smashed around them. She joined in yelling, *"Sa-ku-ra, Sa-ku-ra."*

The wolf turned and loped towards the creek.

"Now, Geechan," Michiko called out. "Run."

Her grandfather dashed to the root cellar, and Sadie pulled him inside.

Michiko dropped the pail and kettle. Her mother lowered the broom. They stumbled inside. When Geechan emerged from the root cellar, Michiko ran to him. He wrapped his arms about her.

"Arigato," he said. *"Arigato, arigato."*

Sadie slammed the trap door shut and heaved several logs onto the coals. Then she stood in front of the stove with her hands on her hips. "I was going to make some tea," she said.

Michiko looked up at her with twinkling eyes. "The kettle is outside." She winked at Geechan and said, "Go and get it."

Seventeen
The Quilt

Monday was washday. Sadie hauled the water from the creek and heated it on the stove. Even though it was winter, she hung the laundry outside. The sheets started out limp, froze stiff then went limp again.

Michiko watched her aunt checking the tea towels for stains at the galvanized tub. Sadie's fingertips were coarse and her nails ragged. With Ted gone, Sadie chopped wood and filled the shed beside the kitchen. Michiko's job was to keep the box beside the stove full.

The wind howled in the eaves and through every chink. The small long-needled pine trembled in its bucket of sand. There was always a slight breeze in the house. Michiko wore her *hanten* over her clothes as she passed the time folding paper cranes as ornaments for the tree.

"I'm going to fold a thousand paper cranes," she announced. "That way my Christmas wish will come true."

Eiko sat at her sewing machine, her hand on the wheel with the needle poised midair, staring straight ahead. There was a ghost of a frown on her face. Her soft brown eyes looked troubled.

Michiko picked up her small pile of finished cranes

and took them to her mother's side. Eiko broke from her reverie. She removed a needle from the red tomato pin cushion and put a thread through the ornament. She tied it off and handed it back.

"Maybe you should make three thousand," Sadie suggested, "just to be sure."

The crane floated and turned about the branch Michiko hung it from. "The tree is too small for three thousand," she said. "We need to leave room for the candles."

"Candles," Sadie scoffed. "The last thing we need is to burn down the house."

Eiko handed Michiko a second threaded crane.

"Can we light just a few candles," Michiko pleaded, "only for a short while?"

"We will see," her mother murmured as she returned to her chair.

There was a knock at the door. Michiko looked at her aunt in surprise before she answered it.

A tall man wearing a leather apron and puttees stood at the front door. A long brown woollen scarf covered his neck below a brown felt cap. A pencil stuck out from behind his ear.

"Your mom home?" he asked. Then he laughed at his own question. "Guess she would be in this weather."

Michiko gasped at what stood behind him. Two huge white dappled horses wearing heavy black studded collars took up most of the road. A long flat blue sleigh bore the letters "CPR" painted in white.

Eiko came up behind. Sadie almost pushed the two of them onto the porch to see.

"Morning, ladies," the carter said, tipping his hat. "Looks like you got a special delivery." He took a folded piece of paper from his jacket pocket and read it. "Is this the Minagawa household?" he asked. He put down a small canvas bag.

"The CPR is the railway," said Sadie in astonishment.

"That's correct, ma'am," replied the carter. "Normally you would have to come down to the station office in Nelson for pickup."

The three of them looked at each other. How could they have managed that?

"Since I was taking the freight sleigh out of town," he explained, "I thought I'd just bring it on up to you. The Clydesdales needed a good run."

"Thank you," Michiko's mother murmured.

The fierce barks of a dog startled them.

The carter turned his head to the sound. "That's Blackie," he explained. "He rides along with me. He guards the freight."

"I guess no one could hitch a ride on the back," Michiko observed.

"Actually, that's not true, young lady." He stepped aside.

Behind him stood Michiko's father.

Michiko rubbed her eyes. A grey wool cap drooped over his dark black hair, and his navy blue coat hung on his frame. The man was pale and thin, but it was her father.

Michiko's mother shrieked, "Sam!" and stepped into his arms. Michiko grabbed his legs, and Sadie clasped his hand. Then she ran inside and called out for Geechan.

"I guess we got the right place," the carter murmured. "Best be on my way."

Sam Minagawa turned to clasp the carter's hand, who then stepped down the wooden steps and headed for the sleigh.

Michiko dragged her father inside. Geechan pulled the blue wicker chair up to the stove and gestured him to sit. He patted Sam on the back several times.

Her mother ran upstairs to wake Hiro.

Sadie poured a cup of steaming tea and pressed the cup into Sam's hands. "Thank you, Sadie," he said and took a great gulp.

"Did you finish building the road through the mountains?" Michiko asked.

Sam gazed at his young daughter before speaking. "Yes, I finished," he said and gazed down into his cup.

Hiro looked at the man in the chair. He turned and buried his face in mother's neck. Then he looked back. Sam cocked his head to one side. "Hello, Hiro," he said with a smile and cocked his head the other way. He smiled again. Hiro broke into a large frown. He turned and buried his face in mother's neck. Sam kissed him on the back of the head. He slumped back into the chair and closed his heavy-lidded eyes.

"They paid us twenty-five cents an hour," he said. He fished in his shirt pocket, brought out a fold of pink bills and tossed it on the table. "Then they took money back for our keep."

No one spoke.

Michiko dragged the quilt from the top of the sewing

machine and tucked it around her father's legs.

"So many nights," he said, "I wished for a quilt like this."

"You wouldn't have wanted this one," Michiko said. "It keeps falling apart."

Her father raised his eyebrows.

"I made this quilt after you left," Eiko informed him. "It is a very special quilt."

Sadie began to giggle. "It is the most valuable quilt in the world." She lifted his hand to one of the red rectangles and said, "Just feel the quality of the material." Sam ran his hand across one of the red silk patches. "Yes," he said, "it is very smooth."

"Now feel," Eiko directed, "I mean, really feel, the quality of the gold patches."

Michiko frowned. What was wrong with her aunt and mother? Why were they making her poor tired father play this silly quilt game? She watched her father rub his hand across one of the gold patches.

"Yes, it is smooth as well," he said tiredly.

"But feel the texture of this one," Sadie insisted. She lifted the corner to him.

Her father rubbed the patch listlessly, but stopped at the sound of a crunch. He grabbed the patch with his hand.

"We sold absolutely everything," explained Sadie.

"Everything?" Sam asked.

"Auntie Sadie even sold her feathered hat," chimed in Michiko, not knowing why.

"We sold the piano, all of the porcelains and the paintings," her mother added. She stopped. Her hand went to her throat, but she didn't say anything about her necklace.

Sam smiled and dropped his hand.

Michiko was glad when this silly game ended. She crept into its folds and put her head on her father's knees. He put his hand on her head and closed his eyes.

Her father was home, Michiko thought. Her family was together once again. She put her hand on top of one of the gold squares. It felt crunchy.

"Why is the quilt crunchy?" she asked.

"There's money inside," her aunt informed her.

"Doesn't money belong in a bank?" Michiko asked. She was confused.

"We don't trust the banks," snapped Sadie, "and if we had, where would we be now?"

Michiko looked at the quilt in amazement. If it was full of money, they could buy anything they wanted. They could buy train tickets back home.

Eighteen
House for Sale

January dragged by. Michiko no longer marvelled at the world of white. There was nothing to do but watch the pale sky, hoping it would soon turn blue.

At daybreak, there was a rap on the front door. "Sadie," a voice called out urgently. Michiko sat up to listen. "Sadie, open up."

Michiko heard the bolt slide back. Sadie must have been waiting. Instantly Michiko was out of her bed. She snatched her grey blanket and pulled over her *hanten*.

The murmur of low voices rose with the dawn as Michiko crept to the top of the stairs. She could see the beam of a flashlight bobbing up and down. What was going on? she wondered.

To her astonishment, the face that she saw in the light, just before it went off, was Ted.

"I was right," Ted whispered. "There's nothing to go back to."

"I already know that," Sadie replied. "Eiko sold everything,"

"That's not what I mean," he barked. "The house is sold."

"What?" her aunt said. "How is that possible?"

"I told you the government would be selling everything off."

"They have no right to do that," Sadie hissed. "Eiko was told the government would look after the house. They said they would be custodians."

"Eggs and vows are easily broken," Ted reminded her in a quiet voice. "My boat was auctioned off long ago."

Movement from her parents' bedroom sent Michiko scurrying back to her room. She tried to bury herself back in sleep but couldn't. All she could think about was the house with the cherry tree in the backyard.

Silently, she said goodbye to the things she thought would be waiting for her.

"Goodbye little top," she said, thinking about the bright red metal sphere that spun when she pulled up the wooden handle and pushed it down. Hiro would have liked to play with that.

"Goodbye tea set," she whispered. Her father's boss, Mr. Riley had given her the set of china cups and saucers with tiny pink floral sprays for Christmas. There were four cups, four saucers and a teapot with a lid. The cream and sugar bowls had little legs, and there were four bright aluminum spoons for each of the saucers. Each cup had "Made in Japan" stamped on the bottom.

Michiko said goodbye to her desk, her crayons, her pencils and even her library card. She lay in her bed thinking of the large room of books with a huge island of a desk in the centre. The large planked floor of polished oak gleamed in the sunlight that streamed from the deep set windows. "Goodbye, library," she whispered. "I don't think I will be back." Finally, she fell back to sleep.

The smell of toast drew her to the kitchen. Michiko climbed on to her father's lap.

"Did you bring me a present?" she asked Ted before she yawned widely.

He reached over and tugged one of her braids. "As a matter of fact, I did." Ted put his hand into his shirt pocket and drew out a long rectangular silver package.

Michiko gasped and put both hands over her heart. It was a bar of chocolate.

"I haven't seen chocolate for months," Sadie murmured.

"There was a time when I tired of the smell of chocolate," Sam commented. "What I would give to be selling it again."

Ted opened the foil and broke the bar into six pieces. "Wet your finger," he instructed Michiko. Then he took hold of it and rubbed it back and forth over one of the squares. Michiko raised her finger to her mouth and sucked it. She smiled. Her finger remained in her mouth even after the chocolate was gone. "If you eat it that way, it will last forever," Ted told her.

"If you eat it this way," said Sadie, popping a square into her mouth, "it's gone."

"If you eat any more," Eiko said, entering the room with Hiro, "you'll spoil your breakfast." Then, to everyone's surprise, she leaned over, picked up a square of chocolate and popped it into her mouth.

Michiko lifted the foil paper and offered a square to her grandfather. He shook his head.

"I'll save it for Clarence," she told him, and he nodded in agreement.

"Who is Clarence?" Sam asked.

Michiko's story of her red-headed friend tumbled out. Her father patted Ted on the shoulders when he heard about the boat and the fishing expeditions. He smiled and nodded at how they'd picked every apple in the orchard and stored them in the root cellar.

Ted got up and pulled on his cap. "I think I'll walk you into town," he told Sadie. He turned to Michiko. "Why don't you come too?" he suggested. "We can visit at the drug store."

Michiko tugged her coat from the wooden peg under the stairs. It had been a dream of hers for some time to visit the drug store. Clarence had told her about the soda fountain.

Despite the drabness of the countryside, Michiko spotted odd bits of colour along the way. The sky was getting bluer, and red tips of the dogwood stood out against the white snow. Michiko smashed the melting ice in the road ruts with her heel as she walked, listening to the conversation.

"How long do you think we will have to stay here?" Sadie asked with a sigh.

"There's nothing wrong with this town," Ted said as they trudged. "The fishing is good."

They walked the rest of the way in silence.

Sadie left them at the tiny church flanked by tall pines. A small sign on the front line read "Teachers Wanted".

Michiko and her uncle walked to the drug store.

Through the window, Michiko could see the glow of the Orange Crush machine fizzing a fountain of golden soda. The five shiny red stools that faced the counter were empty. Pictures of ice cream sundaes plastered the walls. One showed mounds of chocolate, vanilla and strawberry ice cream heaped between slices of banana. Another displayed a tulip-shaped dish, dripping with hot fudge sauce, whipped cream and a fluorescent cherry perched on top.

Ted took a seat. The man behind the counter pushed a small towel along the counter in front of him. Michiko wandered over to the magazine rack.

The bell over the door tinkled, and Michiko looked up to see George.

He spotted her and sauntered over. "Every Saturday, my dad gives me money to buy ice cream," he bragged. He pulled a large glossy magazine from the rack. Michiko glanced at the cover. "I bring this back for my mom," George explained.

Then he lowered his voice. "Don't look now," he cautioned her. "There's a Jap sitting at the counter." He cocked his head in the direction of her Uncle Ted. "He probably just got released from jail."

Michiko turned to look at her uncle in conversation with the man behind the counter. Not everyone in this town thought the way George did. She took a deep breath. "You know that Jap at the counter," she whispered into George's ear.

He learned into her. "Yeah," he whispered and smirked.

"I'm going to sit beside him," Michiko said.

"Yeah," he whispered again. A grin spread across his face. "What are you going to do?"

"I'm going to eat ice cream with him," Michiko told him.

His grin froze.

"He's my uncle," she trilled. "Uncle Ted," Michiko called out. "This is George."

Her uncle spun around on the stool and faced them with a smile.

"Do you remember me telling you about the boy I sit beside at school?"

The smile on Ted's face faded slightly. "Yes, I do," he responded. Then he gestured with an arm. "Would you like to join us for ice cream?" he offered. "It's a special Japanese treat," he added.

George turned scarlet and clutched the magazine to his chest. He scuttled down the aisle like a crab and escaped through the front door.

"Hey," the man behind the soda fountain yelled at the sound of the bell, "you have to pay for that magazine."

"How much is it?" Ted asked, putting his hand in his back pocket. "I'll cover it."

"It's okay," the man replied. "I know who he is." He put down the towel and dish he was drying. "I'll just put it on their tab." Then the man looked at Ted closely. "That was mighty nice of you to offer," he said. "What did you decide to have?"

"Make it a very large banana split," Sadie sang out as the shop bell tinkled again. Her face was bright pink. "We can celebrate my new teaching job." She plunked herself down beside Ted and Michiko. "The woman in charge was very interested in my background in dance."

"When?" asked Michiko.

"They want me to start right away, but I have to be trained first," Sadie informed them. "She suggested I bunk in with one of the teachers at the hotel."

The man behind the counter put a dish of ice cream down in front of Michiko. "Welcome to the big city," he said to Sadie with a smile.

"Good for you," Ted said. "That just leaves the rest of us to find work."

"I could use a hand around here," the man behind the soda fountain said. "Not too many people want to sell ice cream and candy."

"My dad knows more about candy than anyone else in the world," Michiko bragged.

"Well, you better get him in here, if he's looking for a job."

The bell jangled loudly as Michiko tore open the door. She raced down the street. Her dad would be on the road again, but this time he would be walking home every night.

The man at the drug store hired him on the spot. He said they could move into the apartment above the store, if they wanted, since it had been sitting empty for a long time.

Michiko, Ted, Sadie and Sam inspected the rooms over the drug store.

The kitchen had a refrigerator and a toaster. A long tubular water boiler sat next to the range, recessed into a kitchen wall. Sadie touched it with her hand. "No more boiling water on the stove," she sighed. "This is progress."

Michiko raced through the other rooms and came back breathless. "You won't believe it," she said through small short puffs. "There's a bathroom and a piano!" She grabbed Sadie's hand and dragged her towards it.

"I guess they couldn't afford to have it moved," Sadie said, pulling out the small round piano stool with its faded needlepoint seat.

The piano was smaller than the one they'd had at home, made of polished wood. Sadie lifted the key cover and tickled the keys. "It needs tuning of course," she said. She twirled around a few times, making the stool higher. "Your mother will be thrilled with this."

Michiko could see the reflection of her aunt's hands in the dark polished wood. It didn't show their rough redness, but Sadie wouldn't have to worry about her hands if she were teaching.

By the time they returned to the farmhouse, all was decided. Sam, Eiko, Geechan, Michiko and Hiro would live above the store. Sadie would stay at the hotel but eat all her meals with them. Ted would continue to bunk out at the Apple Depot until he got work at the sawmill.

Before bed that night, Michiko took a look at her round face in the window. She picked up the scissors and cut off a pigtail. Then she passed the scissors to Geechan.

It was time for a haircut. She was going to go to that new school in the hardware store. She was proud to be the niece of one of the teachers.

But there was another feeling inside her as well. Because her whole family was together again, she felt grateful.

Japanese vocabulary

In order of appearance in the story

arigato	thank you
Asahi	Japanese baseball team
Baachan	Grandmother
dokodemo	everywhere
furoshiki	bundle made by tying four corners of a square cloth
gangara	hold on, keep going, persevere
Geechan	Grandfather
hanami	spring festival
hanaska-jiisan	old man
hanten	housecoat
haori	long, loose jacket for men
hee-ta	heating
inaka	countrified, farm-like
Issei	first generation, born in Japan
kanji	Japanese system of writing
karate	The art of self-defense
katakana	character symbols for writing syllables
kimono	long, wide-sleeved, elaborately decorated robe
manju	small round rice buns
miso	bean paste, red or white
Momo-Taro	Peach Boy
Nisei	second generation, born outside of Japan

"O-bento?"	"Your lunch?"
ohayo	hello
origami	The Japanese art of paper folding
rakugo	funny story
sakura	cherry
sakura fubuki	cherry blossom snowstorm
sakura-manju	rice buns with cherry filling
shiromuku	white kimono worn by brides
shizukani	"Be quiet!"
shoyu	soya sauce
sunomono	cucumber with vinegar
warabi	green coiled shoots of ferns known as fiddleheads
yakatori	spicy chicken on a stick
yancha	naughty
yasashi	gentle, kind

Born in Niagara Falls, Ontario, Jennifer came from a book-loving family. She worked as a library helper during her summers of public school. Her childhood ambition was to have a book with her name on the spine on the shelves she stacked.

After her retirement as an elementary school principal, Jennifer published short stories for a variety of children's magazines in Canada, Britain and United States. She lives in Mississauga, Ontario, with her husband.